# A DASH OF DESTINY

Warlocks MacGregor®

MICHELLE M. PILLOW®

MichellePillow.com

## About A Dash of Destiny

*A dash of destiny and a pinch of passion can change everything…*

Scottish warlock Rory MacGregor knows something from the supernatural world is trying to kill him. He's not sure exactly what that something is, but it'll make for a fun adventure figuring it all out. Of course, nothing is simple, so when Fate tosses in a dash of destiny to keep him on his toes by way of an enchanting new arrival in town, he's all in.

He just wished she was too.

Life hasn't turned out as planned for Jennifer Greene. After taking care of her sick father for years, she's come to Green Vallis, Wisconsin, for one reason only—a job. She isn't looking for adventure, even if it's by way of a tempting Highlander in a kilt or men streaking across the countryside. And she definitely isn't looking for love—even though love is looking for her.

## Warlocks MacGregor® Series

### SCOTTISH MAGICKAL WARLOCKS

Love Potions
Spellbound
Stirring Up Trouble
Cauldrons and Confessions
Spirits and Spells
Kisses and Curses
Magick and Mischief
A Dash of Destiny
Night Magick

**More Coming Soon**

Visit www.MichellePillow.com for details.

## Author Updates

To stay informed about when a new book is released sign up for updates:

michellepillow.com/author-updates

## Dear Readers

Dear Readers,

It has come to my attention that Uncle Raibeart has been trying to lace all the e-books with love potions. So if you have found yourself waiting and wishing for his proposal, gazing for naked warlocks running past your window with longing, well, we have a support group for that: ~~Michelle M. Pillow Fan Club~~ **Uncle Raibeart Love Fest**!

You can find it online at:
fb.com/groups/MichellePillowFanClub

My sincerest apologies. We do what we can to keep him reined in but unfortunately have not found a proper firewall for Raibeart's magickal hacking skills. If you do see him, please, tell him to put on some clothes and come home. And, whatever you do, do not say yes to anything he proposes.

Thank you,
    Michelle M. Pillow

## Note from the Author

The term "warlock" is a variation on the Old English word "waerloga" primarily used by the Scots. It meant traitor, monster, deceiver, or other variations. The MacGregor Clan does not look at themselves as being what history has labeled their kind. To them, warlock means magick, family, and immortality. This book is not meant to be a portrayal of modern day witches or those who have such beliefs. The MacGregors are a magickal class all their own.

As with all my books, this is pure fantasy. In real life, please always practice safe sex and magic(k).

## Chapter One

IRELAND, 1693

Rory MacGregor watched the muddy hand give one last twitch before the earth swallowed the woman whole. The stitch in his side from trying to push through the peat bog was nothing compared to the agony of defeat. If not for the fact he needed to catch his breath, he would have screamed. Instead, he tried to keep moving in the impossibly thick mud.

His efforts were futile. Rory was knee-deep and sinking. Only too late did he realize his warlock magick was useless in the enchanted trap. For the moment, he was like any other human, imprisoned inside the knowledge that death came for him—in slow, descending inches.

He reached his hand into the bog, feeling

around in a desperate attempt to grab hold of her even though logically, he knew she was too far away. He shivered at the cold pressure against his naked legs. The smell of the decaying plant life stirred each time he slowly tried to lift his foot. This was not the first time he'd been stuck in a bog, but it was the first time he couldn't quickly maneuver his way out of it.

"*Tha mi duilich,*" he whispered to the woman he'd tried to rescue. *I'm sorry.*

Rory knew he should back up, but he tried to take a step forward instead. Her eyes, the same dark color as the land that consumed her, had pleaded with him for help. Maybe if he reached her, there would still be time. The bog refused to release his legs.

Rory glanced around the flat landscape, stretching his neck to see behind him. He caught sight of a figure along the edge of his vision. He tried to twist farther, but the movement caused his body to sink a little more.

"A woman went under," Rory yelled over his shoulder as he pointed to the now-empty bog. "We have to help her!"

He tried to turn, stretching his waist as far as he could. Rory frowned. It was a young lad. A child couldn't help him.

He again attempted to press forward to where

she had gone under. If he could just take a few more steps…

"Get help!" Rory turned to glance back, only to see the boy coming toward him. He couldn't be more than ten years. "No, stop. It's not safe."

The child didn't listen.

"Stop. It's not safe," he repeated, switching to a local dialect. He had no idea how far he'd traveled inland. Ireland was not his homeland, and he did not know the terrain or how close he was to help.

The lad still came forward, his steps sure. The skin on his nose had peeled as if he recovered from too much time in the sun. His brown hair hung in long tangled strands and had not been washed in quite some time.

"Stop," Rory yelled louder, waving his muddy hands for the boy to stay away. From what he could see, the child was alone.

Rory tried to force magick from his fingers to fling the boy back without touching him. Nothing happened.

Rory watched in horror as the lad stepped closer, waiting for him to sink. Miraculously, the ground stayed firm beneath the boy's feet as he circled Rory. He moved as if the bog wasn't waiting to swallow him.

"It's not safe," Rory insisted. He was careful

not to move, not wishing to disturb the earth beneath the boy. "Get help," Rory ordered. The child's luck wouldn't last too long.

The boy stopped behind him. Rory felt small hands on his shoulders. For a second, he thought the child was going to attempt to pull him out.

"Jenny Greentooth," the boy whispered, jumping up to press all of his weight on Rory's shoulders.

Rory lurched, trying to resist as he sank deeper into the bog. On reflex, he pushed his hands in front of him to counteract the attack. His fingers sank beneath the surface. The bog swallowed his waist.

"Och!" He grunted as the peat encased his manhood in its chilly grip.

Rory jerked his hands from the muck and slapped behind his back. The boy laughed as he let go, and Rory heard the child's footsteps running away.

The ground bulged where the woman had gone under, rising and falling as if it breathed. With each lift it grew higher until the surface broke and a peat-covered hand poked through. Dirty fingers slapped the earth.

How was this possible? The woman should be dead.

Rory felt his body sinking deeper.

A second hand appeared. Through the clumps of mud, he detected short claws. The woman pulled herself out of the bog. Though he could pick out small similarities, this creature was not the woman he'd seen disappear.

Peat-covered hair clung to her shoulders. Mud slicked her face and bony arms. A long hiss of breath left her mouth, showcasing rotted teeth marred with decaying leaves. A clump fell from her face, taking what should have been a nose with it.

"Ya must be Jenny," Rory said, not bothering to hide his repulsion as the hag crawled on her stomach from the bog to move along the surface. He struggled to push out of the muck, but the lad had sunk him too deeply.

Jenny smiled, eyeing him like trapped prey she was ready to devour.

"Lovely day for a stroll, isn't it?" Rory had charmed far more dangerous women than her. He gave her his most winning smile.

The bog witch's voice crackled an undistin-guishable answer. Apparently, his charms were lost on Jenny, and she continued toward him.

"Och, this is going to be a tough one," he muttered, unsure what he should do. Panic began to fill him. Without magick he was helpless, and he knew there was no easy escape from Jenny and her enchanted bog.

## Chapter Two

GREEN VALLIS, WISCONSIN, MODERN DAY

When the guidance counselor had sat Jennifer Greene down to talk about her future after high school, waitressing in a small Wisconsin town fifteen years later, living on tips and free employee meals, had not been on her list of dreams. The tater tot nachos at the Crimson Tavern were heavenly, but they weren't health insurance and a 401k.

That was the not-so-funny thing about life. It rarely ended up as intended.

Jennifer had not planned on her mother leaving after a car ran over her older brother. She hadn't imagined her strong father would get so sick he couldn't walk. She hadn't planned on choosing between a college scholarship or a job to take care of him for six years until he succumbed to the big C. She hadn't planned on her friends disappearing from her life one by one by one because they'd moved on and couldn't relate to her struggle. She hadn't planned on her dad's medical bills, a reverse mortgage on her childhood home, or the extremely desperate loneliness that led her into the arms of a man who would leave her when they thought she'd gotten pregnant. It had been a false positive, but the betrayal stung.

*"All it takes is a dash of destiny, and everything can change."*

Her mother told her that the night she left. The look on the woman's face used to haunt her. She'd been so...*excited*. Who could be that happy knowing they were abandoning their child? Jennifer had been six, and it was the only thing she remembered about the woman. She'd thought about those words a lot in her life.

*"All it takes is a dash of destiny..."*

Jennifer stood beside the quiet street outside the Crimson Tavern. Dash of destiny—it sounded like an ingredient in a lousy family recipe. She'd had about all the dashes she could handle. So far, her life's destiny tasted sour and left her more than a little bitter.

Headlights turned off of Main Street and ventured toward her. The downtown streets were constructed of red bricks that had shifted over time to make for bumpy roads. The lights bounced as the slow-moving car neared where she stood close to the Crimson Tavern's door.

The locals treated her like a stranger, but she didn't mind. The solitary hours gave her time to romanticize a make-believe life she was living. A light fog lined the street as if exhaled from windows. The historic buildings squished close together could have been from the 1800s. If she ignored the modern dresses in the store windows, she could pretend she walked through history on the evening streets of London. If she closed her eyes, she could imagine the sound of horse hooves and carriage wheels.

Jennifer lifted her hand to block the headlights as they passed. The bright flash of high beams brought her out of her thoughts and blinded her to who was driving.

Walking alone at night in Green Vallis was relatively safe. The biggest threat was Mrs. Callister, the town gossip, who was always trying to take everyone's pictures. Jennifer was tired of seeing her blurry face on the woman's blog. The woman posted them next to speculation about what *really* went on inside Crimson Tavern.

Waitressing. Waitressing went on. Cheap beer and cheaper come-on lines.

Jennifer spent hours on her feet, fetching burgers, and refilling drinks. It wasn't glamorous, but at least it was honest. She liked honest. It was also boring.

The car turned the corner, and darkness once more covered the street.

"Fifty bucks that was Callister," Kay said from behind her as the door to the building closed slowly. The sound of the spark wheel on the woman's lighter punctuated the words as she attempted to light her cigarette. "Bitch posted a photo of me tripping the other day and insinuated I was drunk. I swear she photoshopped an extra ten pounds on my ass too."

Kay spoke in a gravelly volume even the most foulmouthed of sailors would envy, yet her swearing only seemed to amuse the regulars who came more for the drink than the food. They had worked together for about three months. She took a significant amount of smoke breaks, often leaving Jennifer to pick up the work slack.

"Last week she implied we turn tricks in the storage room." Jennifer picked a piece of fuzz off her shirt and dropped it into the slight breeze. With a sigh, she turned toward the door. Since Kay was outside, that meant no one was watching the tables.

"Yeah, right between the giant cans of

ketchup and extra napkins." Kay laughed. The sound was followed by a cough.

"Under the glow of the swinging light bulb hanging on its wire," Jennifer added.

"You turn on the lights?" Kay laughed harder. "Hell, girl, I charge extra if they want to look at all this."

"We'd be taking home a lot more than fifteen dollars an hour if we were providing extra services." Jennifer opened the door. The fifteen was only after tips on a jam-packed weekend night. The rest of the time, she didn't even want to think about it.

"Too bad none of the MacGregors have been coming in." Kay took a long drag off the cigarette. As she continued, smoke billowed from her lips. "Now there's a few guys I wouldn't mind taking to the storage room."

"Which ones?" Jennifer asked.

"Any of them," Kay said. "As my grandma used to say, they're all fine as frog hair."

"I should get back to it." Jennifer pasted a smile on her face for the customers as she stepped back inside.

She didn't know the MacGregors personally but had heard plenty of gossip about them. A family of kilt-wearing Scottish hotties had moved into the giant house overlooking town a few years ago. They were nobility or hotel moguls or the descendants of the guy who'd invented the vegetable peeler.

She doubted much of it was true. Out of boredom, she'd looked up the inventor of the vegetable peeler. It was a man named Alfred Neweczerzal from Switzerland or some such place. The sexy kilt-wearing part was real. She'd seen a few of the men around town.

One of Kay's customers lifted his hand to get her attention. Several others tried to make eye contact with her. Jennifer let the thoughts slip from her mind as she fell into the rhythm of work.

## Chapter Three

Rory MacGregor wasn't exactly sure what he'd done to deserve his current predicament. The last thing he remembered was having a drink with his cousins Iain, Erik, Euann, and Kenneth. He wasn't sure how they'd gotten on the topic, but they'd been reminiscing about past magickal failures. There were plenty of times a poorly aimed energy ball had boomeranged around to zap one of them in the ass like an errant firework. Literally, the ass. Rory had burnt more than one kilt.

Yeah, he'd done plenty over the centuries, but he didn't know which of those things this was paying back. Was it for the time he'd trapped Iain in an enchanted chicken coop in the 1800s after his cousin had shifted into bird form? Rory had left him there as a human and sold tickets to local farmers to see the chicken-man.

Or was it from several months back, when he'd shot out all of Euann's security cameras in the woods surrounding the MacGregor property for the second time? For a warlock who could cast magickal protection spells, Euann liked playing with tech a little too much.

Rory had convinced a king to let Kenneth sing opera for the royal court. But, to be fair, that was only because Kenneth had stolen his kilt while he'd been swimming and left him with a woman's dress. So Rory had been the one to repay that particular prank.

He'd enchanted Erik's car. And his horse. And his sword. And, well, also his boxer shorts.

Maybe it was because he'd helped himself to Uncle Raibeart's not-so-secret stash of old scotch. That had been a fun couple of nights.

He'd dyed Uncle Fergus's English bulldog pink. Traitor hadn't seemed to mind his new coloring. In fact, Traitor didn't mind much of anything.

The list was endless. Pranks were a MacGregor family trademark. Whatever the reason, Rory was pretty much screwed until this spell wore off.

Rory tried to stretch his arms and legs. The

rope binding him to the tree held firm with the help of magick. They contained some kind of binding spell that kept his magick inert. If he struggled, the binds would only become tighter. As far as revenge went, this wasn't so bad. The temperature was mild, and the air fresh. Moonlight came through the treetops to create dancing spots on the forest floor.

Soft thumps sounded on the nearby path. Maybe he'd dismissed the vulnerability of this prank too soon.

Rory tensed, wondering what shenanigans his cousins had planned for him. He tried to wriggle free, but the binds tightened, causing the bark to rub uncomfortably against his flesh. That's when he realized nothing protected his bare ass from the tree.

Of course, he was naked beneath the ropes. Why wouldn't he be? It would be funnier to make him run nude through the forest back to the mansion where he lived with his extended family.

The ropes kept his body stationary so he could only turn his head to watch. A tiny black ball of fluff barreled down the path. At first, he wasn't sure if it was a dog or a miniature bear cub.

"Arf," came a high-pitched bark.

The puppy tripped over his feet, rolling head-first before continuing without barely missing a beat. This prank just became weird. Were his cousins trying to cute him to death?

"Come back. Where'd you go, little guy?"

He didn't recognize the soft American-accented voice. A woman appeared from between two trees, her face downturned as she searched along the narrow path. "It's not safe for you here. Let's find your home. Someone has to be worried about you."

Rory held very still, hoping his current trap included an invisibility spell so she wouldn't see him. Leaving someone tied up and helpless in a forest was hilarious, to be sure, but they weren't stupid. His cousins would not have left him without protection.

As expected, the woman glanced through him, not registering the fact someone had tied him to the tree. Her dark curly hair was pulled back from a pretty face. Exhaustion lined her eyes, and she looked like she hadn't slept for days.

Rory wanted to call out to her but held back. If she heard him, she'd think the forest was haunted and would run away screaming in fear.

Something in her expression captured him. Sadness lined her eyes. He wanted to know why she looked that way. She was too young, probably only thirty or so human years, to look so forlorn.

The woman rubbed her arms as she looked

into the trees for the dog. "Please come back. Tips sucked tonight. My feet are killing me. I'm bone tired. I want to go home and collapse, but I can't leave you out here."

"Arf," came the high-pitched, slightly muffled answer.

The woman crouched down as she took a few steps to search the darker part of the woods. Rory's binds tightened as he tried leaning his head to the side to get a better look at her ass beneath the black slacks. She kneeled and reached forward. The pants pulled tighter. Rory's lips parted, and he suppressed a groan to keep from making noise.

"There you are," she said, sitting back on her heels.

Rory sighed and rested his head against the tree trunk.

At the sound, the woman quickly turned as if she'd heard him.

He'd expected a puppy, but instead, metal glimmered in her hand. Her eyes met his. Dark circles spread from her eyes like bruises bleeding across the flesh.

She slowly stood, wielding a knife. "There you are."

The sweet concern she had for the lost puppy

had drained from her tone. Her body twitched as she stepped toward him.

Well, this evening soured fast.

"Oh, easy there, love," Rory said. "Whatever this is, I'm sure we can talk about it. Why don't ya put the knife on the ground before someone gets hurt?"

She lifted the knife over her shoulder and aimed it in his direction. So much for conversation. The woman hardly seemed receptive.

Rory tried to call forth his magick, but whatever enchantment was on the ropes kept him imprisoned. A distant memory tried to surface, of being trapped and powerless, but after hundreds of years of living, there were many strange events to choose from, and the impression faded as fast as it came.

"Did one of my cousins put ya up to this?" he asked. Only to yell, "Hilarious guys, but you're going to have to do better than this!"

"There you are," she whispered, taking another halting step toward him. Her eyes bored into him as if she could pierce him with a single look. Mounting rage replaced the sadness in her. The grip on the knife hand shook.

"I think maybe ya got the wrong guy." Rory wasn't usually one to panic, but he couldn't see a way out. His heartbeat quickened, and a bead of sweat rolled down his temple. "How about ya untie me instead? We can get a bite to eat and talk about this?"

"There you are."

Stupid ropes.

Rory struggled to free himself even as the bind became so tight it began cutting off his circulation. He tried to pull energy from the tree behind him to fuel his magick. A small tingle worked down his spine, but it wasn't enough to make even the lamest of fireballs.

"There you are."

"Aye, here I am," he answered.

"There you are." Her voice crackled, and a strange sound popped in the back of her throat as she cocked her arm farther back.

"Ha-ha! Very funny guys," Rory yelled, hoping his cousins would jump out of the trees at any moment.

"There you are." The woman screeched and lunged.

Rory cried out and shut his eyes tight as he braced for impact. A loud thud sounded. His body tried to jerk, but the ropes held him. He waited for the sharp pain of her blade.

"Och, laddie, what did ya do to put the hornet in this one's bonnet? She looks ready to skin ya."

Uncle Raibeart's voice brought with it a wave of relief.

Rory opened his eyes and frantically looked around. The woman laid face down on the ground. Her arm was outstretched over her head, but the knife had fallen from her fingers.

"I didn't know ya were into bondage." Raibeart appeared before him with a grin. Not surprisingly, his uncle was buck-ass naked. Raibeart placed his hand on his hips. "Didn't mean to interrupt your date. She should come to in like six, seven hours. I'll leave ya to it."

Raibeart started to leave.

"Raibeart, wait," Rory yelled. It was no secret that his uncle wasn't all there. The way he'd heard the story, Raibeart had been involved with an *inthrall*. *Inthralls* were human women, but for some reason, they were able to tap into a warlock's power—not all warlocks; the match had to be perfect, so it was extremely rare. Raibeart's lover drained his magick and left him a few clubs short of a golf game.

Raibeart returned. "Ya haven't seen a troll run by here, have ya? He stole my favorite tutu."

A troll stealing his uncle's clothing would not be the reason Raibeart was running around naked. More security cameras had spotted the man's bare ass streaking than anyone in the family cared to know about.

"Untie me," Rory ordered. It had become difficult to breathe, and he fought a wave of dizziness.

"Ya are a demanding…" Raibeart grumbled. "No wonder your woman tried to stab ya. For future knowledge, laddie, when ya are tied up, you're the submissive. That's how these games work."

A flash of blue lit up the forest seconds before it slammed into Rory's chest. His breath knocked out of him. "Oof!"

The ropes didn't budge, and Raibeart tried a second time, zapping Rory with a more potent dose of magick.

"Ow, stop!" Rory cried.

Raibeart hit him a third time, then a fourth.

"Ow, Raibeart, stop. The ropes are enchanted. That's not working." Rory flinched as he waited for a fifth blast that didn't come.

"Why didn't ya say so?" Raibeart came to stand in front of him.

"I tried. Ya keep hitting me," Rory countered.

"Ya asked me to." Raibeart looked at the unconscious woman on the path. "She's just a wee little thing, isn't she? How did she convince ya to stand still long enough to truss ya up?"

"I didn't let her," Rory protested.

"And yet there ya are." Raibeart laughed. "What did ya do to piss off this one?"

"Nothing. She just attacked." Rory fought for each breath and talking was not easy. "I don't even know who she is."

Raibeart chuckled as he leaned over and picked up the knife the woman had dropped. "How many times do I have to tell ya boys? Women don't like it when ya forget their names."

"This coming from a man who forgets the women he's asked to marry him," Rory mumbled.

"Hey," Raibeart pointed the knife tip at him to enunciate his words. "I have a plan."

"Plan?" Rory's hands and feet tingled. "Can that plan please include cutting me free? I am losing feeling in my limbs."

"The woman I'm meant to be with will say aye to me," Raibeart explained, even though Rory didn't ask him to. "I had a conversation with Fate once and learned a few things. I'm playing my odds."

"Sure. That sounds sane." Rory couldn't keep the sarcasm from his voice. "No way that could backfire on ya."

"Ya would be wise to do the same," Raibeart advised. "Only, maybe not this one. She doesn't seem to like ya very much. But she's pretty. I might ask her when she wakes up. I gave her quite a stun, so it might be a while before she can answer."

"Aye, six or seven hours, ya said," Rory said between gritted teeth. "I'm losing feeling in my manhood."

"That can't be too pleasant." Raibeart gave a dramatic shiver. "Never liked constriction myself."

"Cut me free. Now. Please, now." Rory fought for consciousness. The world was beginning to feel a little wobbly. His head drooped forward.

He felt tiny vibrations as Raibeart began sawing at the rope with the blade. The pressure on his chest eased, and he was able to inhale deeply.

"Enough games. Which one of ya tied me up with enchanted rope and sent this woman after me?" Rory asked, keeping an eye on the unconscious woman. "The last thing I remember was drinking earlier with all of ya earlier tonight."

"That was two days ago. Your ma has been worried about ya, laddie." Raibeart sawed faster. "Ya went to take a shower after ya spilled your liquor and didn't come back out. Since a man can only play with himself for so long, we decided we'd better check on ya. The water was running cold, and it looked like ya had just melted down the drain. I told them not to worry. Sometimes a man has to run free, but ya know how the chickens gobble."

The grip around his body broke free. Rory leaned forward. The rope slithered from around him, releasing him so that he fell onto his hands and knees. He took several deep breaths, willing the blood to flow through his limbs. The sensation of pins and needles prickled in places he'd rather not have such an unpleasant feeling.

"I don't know who the mystery date is, but she has good taste in knives. I haven't seen a scian this pretty since we raided that stronghold. Ya know the one," Raibeart said.

"Actually, no, I don't." Rory crawled a few steps to get a better look at the woman's face.

"Sure ya do. The Saxons had us pinned," Raibeart said. "And someone, I'm not saying who, bespelled their clothing to run away. It was a chilly march home that autumn."

"I have no idea what you're talking about," Rory said though the story sounded vaguely familiar. It seemed like something from his elders' younger days.

"Were ya not there?" Raibeart shrugged. "It matters not. If we have to slay her, can I keep the scian for my collection?"

"We are not slaying anyone," Rory denied.

The woman looked as if she'd been beaten.

He had seen her eyes bruise, untouched by any physical hand. Magick was at play here, and that magick—for some unknown reason—wanted him dead.

But why?

Rory didn't personally have a lot of enemies that he knew about. He usually left the supernatural hunting to his cousin Niall if he could help it. As a werewolf and a warlock, Niall's temper was better suited to the lifestyle. Yes, the MacGregor family as a whole had enemies, but he wasn't exactly the highest target on that list. If he had to fight, he would, but he saw no reason to seek out danger.

The town of Green Vallis had been built on powerful ley lines. It was that nexus of power that called out his family, but it also lured other supernaturals. Not all of them had honorable intentions. Could it be something new had come to town to threaten him and his family?

"Do ya think she's a warlock hunter?" Rory asked, trying to make sense of the attack. "Do ya think someone is using her to get to us?"

"Us?" Raibeart shook his head. "She wasn't trying to get me. The ladies love me."

"Can ya turn off your Raibeartness for a moment and help me figure this out?" Rory insisted. "She almost killed me. I would think that would warrant a little concern on your part."

"But she didn't," Raibeart dismissed as if it were no big deal. Rory had to wonder about his uncle sometimes. The family accepted that he was off, but lately, it had been getting worse. "Why would I worry? I told ya. I talked to Fate. This was not your time."

"Fate told ya when I was going to die?" Rory asked. "And ya didn't think that information was worth sharing?"

"Knowing when ya will perish is not a blessing," Raibeart said. "It's an expiration date ya spend your life marching toward. I would not wish that on anyone."

"But knowing also gives people a chance to make sure their affairs are in order," Rory countered. "When did this Lady Fate tell ya I was going to die?"

How could he not ask?

"Uh, let me think, seventeen…"

"The seventeenth of what?" Rory prompted. He stared at the woman's chest, watching it rise and fall with breath. Relief filled him. She was alive, unconscious, but alive. Whatever quarrel she had with him, they had time to figure it out.

"Seventeen ninety-eight." Raibeart gave a decisive nod. "That's your date."

"Fate told ya I was to die in seventeen ninety-eight?" Rory frowned at his uncle.

"Aye."

"So I am going to die two hundred and twenty-some years in the past?"

"Aye."

"So now we can time travel?"

"Not sure. It was *Fate*. I didn't question her predictions," Raibeart frowned. "That would have been rude."

"Did fate happen to be buying drinks during happy hour?" Rory rubbed the bridge of his nose.

"So you've met her?" Raibeart grinned. "They didn't call it happy hour back then, and I was doing the buying. It was the only way to get her to talk."

This wasn't the first time Raibeart received questionable information from a drunk at a bar. Fate was probably a buxom seventeenth-century prostitute named Brunhilda who'd found an easy mark in his rich uncle's imagination.

"Materialize some clothes." Rory stood. "We don't want her waking up to two naked men standing over her." He gestured his hand down his body, magickally calling forth a kilt to wrap around his hips. Thank goodness he had his magick back. That had been a strange feeling being so defenseless.

Raibeart stayed naked. "I zapped her good. She's going to be out for a while."

So he kept saying, but there was no guarantee.

"Raibeart, please," Rory pleaded.

"The garden troll chewed holes through my favorite kilt," he said. "I'm waiting for your ma to fix it."

"Then wear your second favorite," Rory said, exasperated. "I swear you're worse than Jewel sometimes."

Jewel was Kenneth's daughter. She'd been born with unlimited power, and she used it as any toddler would—to force everyone into playing tea party and princess fashion show with her. Like all the men in his family, Rory knew he'd been blessed with a handsome face. However, he wasn't sure any person could look good impersonating a cake topper in giant petticoats and chafing taffeta.

"Don't make me regret saving ya," Raibeart warned. "That Jewel is a blessing."

Rory kneeled beside the woman and slipped his arms under her. She moaned as he lifted her from the ground. "Which way back to the manor?"

Raibeart had a horrible sense of direction, so Rory fully intended to walk the opposite way.

"We can't take her to the manor." Raibeart shuffled his feet back and forth, thrusting the knife into the air at an imaginary foe. "Your ma and Margareta won't like ya bringing trouble into the house. They just refinished the floors after someone let the gremians in."

"That was ya who let the gremians in," Rory said.

"Aye, and they weren't happy about it," Raibeart maintained.

"We can't leave her here." Rory shifted her in his arms. "Do ya see a purse anywhere? Maybe she has a wallet with her address. With luck, she'll think tonight was a weird dream."

Raibeart dipped to look underneath her body as he searched the area. He picked up a rolled black cloth and dug inside. "Got an apron."

"What's in it?"

"Pen. Notepad with an order for six hamburgers. Wad of cash. Mostly ones." Raibeart put everything back into the apron and rolled it up. "No ID. No phone." He deposited the apron onto the woman's stomach. "I could go for six hamburgers. Ya hungry? You're buying."

"We can't leave her out here. I'll take her to the motel. Maura will let me use one of the rooms." Rory's sister and brother had recently purchased the local motel. Ironically, the last owner had named Hotel in the misguided hope that it would trick people into thinking it was classier than it was. Whenever the MacGregors moved to a new town, they intended to buy up as many local businesses and properties as possible. Control over a city made it easier to keep their magick a secret. Also, it boosted local economies and gave the family members something to ease the boredom of eternity.

"Right," Raibeart drawled sarcastically. "I have to put on a kilt to hide my glory but waking up in a motel with a strange man won't scare her."

"I'm not going to stay in the room with her," Rory denied. "I am a gentleman."

"Since when?" his uncle snorted.

"She'll be safe at the motel. When she wakes up, I'll have a civil conversation with her and find out why she's upset with me."

Raibeart nodded and went to pick up the enchanted rope, winding it around his arm. "This should hold her while we get answers."

"We're not tying her up." Rory peered into the trees. He gestured the best he could and said, "Reveal yourself."

Tiny blue lights rose from the ground, small pinpoints marking where living creatures were around them.

The largest light source danced over Raibeart, who laughed. "Oo tickles."

The simple spell revealed what was probably a

deer in the forest and several smaller woodland animals. Seeing the light coming from low on the ground, Rory nodded his head in its direction. "She was chasing a puppy when she came across me. Would ya mind rescuing the poor thing so we can find it's home?"

Raibeart's expression turned serious at his mission. "Aye. Leave it to me."

Rory carried the woman down the path the way she'd come hoping it would lead them to town. He looked at her calm face. She appeared to be resting. "Let's figure out where we are and get ya to safety."

## Chapter Four

The last thing Jennifer expected to see when she opened her eyes was a fat cherub statue smiling down at her in front of red-and-gold striped wall-paper. Her arms felt heavy like she'd been given a sedative. For a moment, she stared at the chubby cheeks and obnoxiously cute smile, waiting for the dream to end.

*Any second now…*

*Any second…*

*What the…?*

Jennifer screamed as full reality came over her, and she flailed into action. Her limbs tangled in the bedding, and she kicked and punched at them until they let her go. In her wild flight, she slid off the side of the bed. She crawled toward a motel room door, next to a window with drawn curtains.

"Oh, crap."

A woman's surprised voice behind her propelled Jennifer into further action. She pushed up from the floor and lurched for escape. In her panic, she yanked the doorknob so hard that the door smacked her in the knee. Pain radiated up her leg, buckling it beneath her. She grabbed the doorframe to keep from tripping.

"Wait, please."

It was then she registered the woman had a Scottish accent.

Where the hell was she?

Jennifer blinked as the bright light of morning streamed over her face. Cars filled a motel parking lot. She kept hold of the doorframe for support as she turned to see who was behind her.

A woman stood, arms lifted to the side, fingers spread to show she meant no harm. Her short red hair looked wet, and droplets trailed down her temples as if she'd run the facet over her head. Tiny drops darkened the material of her green t-shirt. "My name is Maura MacGregor. You're safe. You're in a room in my motel. We couldn't find any ID on ya, so we weren't sure where ya lived."

"I…" Jennifer looked from the red-and-gold room to the parking lot. "Is this…?"

"What?"

"A pay-by-the-hour type of motel?" Jennifer asked. "Are you a…?"

"A madam?" Maura laughed, dropping her arms. She looked around the room. "I told Bruce his romantic-honeymoon room theme was a bad idea. It looks more boom-chicka-boom than congratulations-on-your-new-marriage. But if ya think this is bad, ya should have seen the horror-movie theme he had planned. I told him no one would want to stay somewhere with a creepy-ass clown hanging over the bed."

Jennifer automatically looked up at the ceiling. Cherubs hung off the light fixture. One of them pointed a golden arrow at her. She doubted anyone would ask to sleep under those creepy things willingly, either.

"What am I doing here? How did I get here?" Jennifer stayed in the doorframe, half in the room, half out.

"Do ya remember anything from last night?" Maura asked.

"I was walking home, and I found…" She frowned. Had she been attacked? There was a dark spot in her memory. "I was following something."

"Your puppy? We found the little guy hiding in the trees. A couple of the maids have been keeping him company, playing with him so ya could rest."

"I don't have a puppy," Jennifer said, yet she had the vague impression of trying to stop a little ball of fur from getting lost in the forest. She remembered thinking she would take him to the shelter where, hopefully, they would have someone who could take care of him. "I can't afford a pet."

Though she was glad to hear, the little fellow was all right.

"We should probably call the animal shelter and see if anyone is missing him," Jennifer said. "And if not…"

"I'll take care of it. My family does a lot of fundraising for the shelter," Maura answered. "We'll see if we can find his owners, but if we can't, I promise ya we'll look after him."

"Thank you." Jennifer wished she could keep the little runaway but knew it was kinder to let him go to a home with a yard and people who could care for him.

"Do ya recall anything else?" Maura asked.

Another image flickered through her mind, that of glowing hands and balls of light. "Nothing that makes sense."

"What doesn't make sense?" Maura prodded.

Jennifer shook her head, refusing to answer. "I don't understand how I came to be here."

"My brother and uncle found ya in the woods. They brought ya here to rest." Maura crossed over to the dresser to lift something from the top. "They said ya had this apron with ya."

Jennifer flinched and pushed into the door-frame when Maura tried to come closer. The protective action was more a reflex than anything. Maura stopped and slowly set the apron on the corner of the bed before backing away.

"They didn't find a cellphone," the woman said.

"I rarely take it to work with me." No one ever called Jennifer except for work.

Jennifer looked at the apron, knowing she needed the money she had inside and yet unwilling to go fully back into the room to pick it up.

"Was I attacked?" Jennifer felt her head for injury. It still felt fuzzy. "Robbed?"

"I don't think so," Maura said. "There is still money in your apron. I couldn't find anything wrong with ya. Maybe ya passed out?"

Jennifer did a mental inventory of her body. Thankfully, she didn't feel like someone violated her. However, that didn't account for the heaviness in her limbs and the dullness impeding her thoughts. She glanced outside, not seeing anyone

MICHELLE M. PILLOW®

in the motel parking lot. "Why here? Why not a hospital? Or call the police?"

Maura's explanation seemed to be lacking. If Jennifer had found someone passed out in the forest, she would have called for help. There is no way she would have dragged that person, unconscious, to a motel to sleep off a hangover and hope for the best. They weren't in the backwoods away from civilization. This was a town, with doctors and police officers and an ambulance service. The only reason people didn't call for help was if they were hiding something.

Maura's smile remained intact, but her eyes shifted away and then back.

"I can't come up with a good answer for that," Maura said at length. "I suppose because we didn't think ya needed one. It's probably a good thing too. If ya can't afford a puppy, I doubt ya can afford an emergency room visit for exhaustion."

Maura wasn't wrong.

"My family was never big on visiting hospitals," Maura continued. "My ma has always been a bit of a natural healer. Her name is Cait MacGregor. I can call her if ya want. She lives up on the hill in the family manor. Won't charge ya to look ya over."

Jennifer couldn't say she blamed them for that.

She hated hospitals. The smell of disinfectants barely hiding the sickness beneath. Unoffensive pictures of flowers in vases and meadow-filled landscapes hanging on light pastel walls. They were supposed to induce a calming effect. Sound breaking through the long silences was the worst part—monitor beeps or soft moans of pain.

The grief that hit her came in an unexpected wave. All these years later and thinking of her father's last days could still knock her to her knees. He was the only person who had ever loved her. Well, that wasn't fair. Her brother had probably loved her, but they had been siblings, bickering more than connecting.

"Do ya need a doctor?" Maura's smile had fallen. She came forward, reaching out.

Jennifer pressed harder against the doorframe. The memory of glowing hands tried to surface. Her thoughts lagged. "I think I need coffee."

"That, I can provide." Maura picked up the apron from the bed and gestured that Jennifer should leave first. "We should have coffee in the office."

They walked along the shaded sidewalk past the row of motel room doors. In the distance, the sound of a nail gun shot in a steady rhythm.

"Ya have a name?" Maura asked. "I feel like I should have something to call ya."

"Oh, uh, Jennifer Greene." Jennifer glanced around the parking lot. She couldn't shake the feeling of being watched.

"Lived here long?"

"Not really."

"What made ya choose Green Vallis?"

Jennifer knew the woman was trying to make polite conversation. Still, considering she'd just woken up in a place that she didn't remember going to, talking about her geographical history was weird.

"It's not a very exciting story," she answered. "I had a job delivering for a bakery. Green Vallis was on my route. When word came that they were cutting back distribution, I happened to be here and saw a help-wanted sign for a waitress position at Crimson Tavern. I interviewed, and the owner offered it to me. Since having a job is better than not, I accepted. I finished my last run, drove my delivery van back, then loaded my stuff to move here. Jefferson, the owner, hooked me up with a Dale Coldwater, who had a trailer I could rent."

Maura nodded but didn't speak.

"I told you it wasn't exciting," Jennifer said. "What about you? Have you lived here long?"

"Not very," Maura said. As if realizing she still had Jennifer's apron, she handed it over.

"And what made *you* choose Green Vallis?"

Jennifer fingered the apron's contents, feeling the wad of cash and the heavier weight of change she'd made in tips the night before.

"I didn't have much of a choice. The MacGregor clan tends to stick together, maybe a little too much. My cousin, Erik, discovered this town and bought the mansion on the hill—have ya seen it?"

Jennifer nodded. "Only from a distance. I overhear customers talking about it a lot."

"Well, the mansion is huge, which was one of the reasons the family purchased the property. The elders moved in. My cousins moved in, and my brother Rory. Then my cousins' new wives moved in. And, well, there are a lot of relatives living up in that madhouse. Technically, I have a room there too, but I prefer to spend most of my time down here with the normal folk." Maura pushed at the door labeled "Front Desk" and held it open for Jennifer. A ringing phone greeted them.

"Normal folk?"

Maura didn't respond to her question as she went to answer the motel phone.

Jennifer came from what essentially had been a family of two. She used to daydream about what it would be like to have a giant family—people always coming in and out, barbeques in the park, parties in the backyard, endless birthdays, and even bickering over the holiday turkey. Beyond that, she would wish she had someone to call during those times when taking care of her father had kept her up for days at a time, and all she'd wanted for herself was a four-hour nap.

Or to stand beside her listening to the doctors in case she missed something.

Or someone else to plan the funeral.

Or to come to the funeral, so she didn't have to sit alone.

"Yes, sir, nonsmoking," Maura said into the phone. "Yes, I have ya down for the twentieth."

Jennifer half-listened to Maura's call as she booked a guest. The front lobby was small but newly painted. A rack of brochures for local sights hung on the wall. There was even one for Crimson Tavern with a picture of tater tot nachos. The image made her think of the night before. They'd had a party of seven show up late, which made her shift last longer. It would have been fine except they'd tipped her a dollar apiece—seven bucks for two extra hours of waiting on a one-hundred-thirteen-dollar tab.

*Assholes.*

After her shift, she'd walked home. A puppy had run in front of a passing car, almost getting hit. She'd chased after the animal to keep it safe, knowing it was stupid to cut off the path and go into the woods alone at night. Then…

Glowing hands.

That was it. Glowing freaking hands.

"All right, sir. Will do. Uh-huh. Ya too." Maura hung up the phone.

"I thought people booked online these days," Jennifer said.

"Some guests like talking to people instead of machines," Maura answered as she finished typing on the computer. She scratched behind her ear. "What were we talking about? Oh, yeah, my crazy family in the mansion."

"Who are ya calling crazy?" A man came from the back room.

Jennifer stiffened at the sight of him. Even without the Scottish accent, he looked related to Maura. Blond highlights tipped his brown hair, and though neatly cut, it stuck up in a messy style. The lobby felt even smaller with him in it. The air seemed to pull out of the room, and she took an unsteady breath.

The man's green eyes met hers. A charming smile graced his lips, but his eyes carried a different emotion, a question she didn't know how to answer. Seeing him filled her with mixed feelings. He wore a tight black t-shirt and a kilt—*a freaking kilt!*—that showed off his calves and knees.

As a single woman who had no prospects for a boyfriend, she instantly noted his attractiveness. The man was doable, in the crassest sense of the word.

Her attraction wasn't what alarmed her. That much was to be expected. It was the seed of rage that tried to grow. There was an itch inside her hands to punch that smile from Rory's face.

Seriously, what the heck?

First, she had no reason to want to injure a stranger. Second, she didn't punch people. Third, what was happening to her?

"Bloody hell, Rory, stop staring at the poor girl," Maura scolded. "This is my new friend, Jennifer. Jennifer, ignore my brother. For some reason, he was born without manners. I begged ma to trade him for a pony, but for some reason, she kept him."

Friend? Aside from Kay at work, that was the first time anyone in Green Vallis had used the word in relation to her. And Kay only used it when she wanted something.

"Jennifer?" Maura asked. "Everything all right?"

Jennifer made a weak noise and nodded. "Sorry, I'm a little pre-coffee." She pushed the rage down and took a deep breath. It did little to calm the emotion. "So, Maura's brother? You're responsible for the cupid room?"

"Oh, hell no," Rory denied. "That's my brother, Cory."

"Cory and Rory?" she repeated.

Another man joined them from the back.

"My name is Bruce. *Not* Cory." Rory's identical twin might have looked like his brother, but his hair and manner of dress were completely opposite.

Rory looked like he had biweekly visits to the barber and took time picking out his clothes. Bruce appeared to have rolled out of bed and just grabbed what was closest. Colorful swatches of paint had dried on his hands. They weren't colors she would expect to see on motel walls.

"Cory and Rory sound like the opening act to *Howdy Doody*," Bruce added. "Nice to meet ya, Jennifer. Welcome to Hotel Motel."

"We're changing the name," Maura said. "Hotel Motel is stupid."

"I think it has charm," Bruce said. "Kind of an ironic play on class perception. What makes a hotel better than a motel? Or is a motel better? And why do we feel the need to make such distinctions? What do ya think, Jennifer?"

"I think…" Jennifer felt as if there was a conversation happening beneath the surface that she wasn't privy to hearing. Or, she needed that coffee. Whatever was happening, she saw them all looking at her for an answer, and she felt compelled to say something smart. "I think for some reason motels remind me of a 1950s road trip, or the Bates Motel."

Well, if not smart, at least honest.

"Oh—" Bruce began in obvious excitement.

"No," Maura interrupted, lifting her hand to cut off her brother's idea before it even formed. "Ya are not making a *Psycho*-themed suite. Your damned cherubs already sent Jennifer screaming from the room. I told ya no one wants to wake up to Cupid's butt in their face."

"It's a play on the commercialization of romance," Bruce explained. "Like Valentines Day."

"What you're saying is the cherub suite has nothing to do with the fact a cherub shot Rory in the ass at Euann's wedding," Maura replied.

"Hey," Rory protested.

"Best Christmas card ever." Bruce laughed.

"You must be an artist," Jennifer surmised.

Bruce lifted his paint-covered hands and grinned. "What gave it away?"

Jennifer glanced at Rory. He smiled, and his eyes still questioned. He didn't say anything to her, merely watched.

"So, I have to ask. Is there a reason people call you Cory? Or is it just a rhyming nickname?" Jennifer glanced around for a coffeepot. The fog in her head had started to clear but could use a little help.

"No reason," Bruce answered.

"Yes, reasons," Maura corrected. "We call him that for a couple of reasons. First, because he dressed like a certain actor in the 1980s—there was a lot of gel and makeup involved. It was quite tragic."

"And second?" Jennifer asked.

"Because it irritates him," Rory said with a grin.

A chill worked over her at the sound of his voice. Her right hand shook before tightening into a fist. Jennifer grabbed the fist with her free hand and pried the fingers open.

"Which one of you found me?" Jennifer asked, staring at Rory. "Or is there another brother?"

"I did, with my uncle Raibeart," Rory answered.

Was the reason she was so angry with him in that knowledge somewhere?

Jennifer knew she should thank him, but she couldn't force the words out of her mouth. "What were you doing in the woods?"

"Night stroll," he said.

She felt he was lying to her.

She also had no proof of it.

When she didn't comment, he continued, "When we found ya, ya weren't making much sense. I honestly thought ya were drunk, so we brought ya here to sleep it off."

"Drunk," she repeated, doubtful. She couldn't drink at work.

"Ya smelled like it," Rory said.

Jennifer automatically looked at her work shirt and sniffed. Sure enough, she smelled like stale liquor. One of the cheap asses from the table of seven had spilled his whiskey on her. "I wasn't drunk."

"Jennifer was wondering why no one thought to take her to the hospital," Maura told her brother.

"It was late, and we thought ya just needed rest. Maybe we should have," Rory said. "I'm sorry if ya think we didn't do right by ya. I did ask my sister to keep an eye on ya. I didn't want ya waking up in a motel room with a man hovering nearby. I'll take ya to a hospital now if ya require a doctor. Or our ma is a healer."

"Maura told me," Jennifer said.

"Our ma's cheaper," Maura added.

"Free," Bruce corrected. "Ma don't charge."

"I don't need a healer," Jennifer stated.

"That's right. We were getting ya coffee." Maura turned to head toward the back.

"Out," Bruce said.

"What?" Maura frowned at him.

"We're out of coffee. Ya need to go to the store," Bruce answered.

"*I* need to go to the…" Maura arched a brow and crossed her arms over her chest. She was shorter than her brothers, but Bruce instantly straightened his shoulders.

"I was just about to go to the store," he said.

Maura nodded. "That's what I thought ya were saying."

"It's all right. I should head home. I have a double shift today," Jennifer said. There were too many people in the small lobby, and she couldn't get rid of the urge growing inside her to attack Rory.

"Hey, go buy her a coffee and drop her off, would ya?" Maura said to Rory. "There is no reason to make her walk."

"I'll be fine," Jennifer stated.

"I don't mind." Rory instantly went to the door and opened it for her. "I'd love to take ya for coffee."

His tone dipped, and he made it sound like they were about to go on a date. Jennifer glanced down at her smelly shirt. "I'm…"

"Perfect," Rory grinned.

Jennifer glanced at Maura, who nodded enthusiastically at her.

"Okay," Jennifer agreed. "Thanks."

"Since you're working tonight, I'll stop by to try those nachos I keep hearing about," Maura said. "I haven't been there yet."

Jennifer smiled. She genuinely enjoyed Maura and Bruce's conversation. They were friendly and easy to like. She wanted to like Rory, but something inside her tried to explode each time she looked at him. She couldn't figure out why. His smile was kind. Objectively, she could say he was handsome. He didn't stare at her chest or make inappropriate comments. There was nothing untoward she could put her finger on.

And still, she wanted to deck him.

When she walked by him, she detected the faintest trace of cologne. He stood against the door, holding it open. It caused her to pass close to him, and she noticed the heat radiating from his body. She felt the warmth inside her as if it tried to soothe the coldness of the rage she suppressed. None of her emotions made sense.

Rory moved past her into the parking lot. She stood on the sidewalk, cradling her apron against her waist while deciding what she should do.

Finally, she jogged a few paces until she fell into step next to him.

"Do you mind if we make the coffee drive-thru? I don't want to go in anywhere," she said. "Not smelling like I work in a bar."

He actually looked a little disappointed, and she again had the impression this was some kind of a strange date for him.

"Sure. We can do that," Rory answered.

The 1966 black Mustang that he led her to looked as if he'd driven it off the lot that very morning. She knew it was a '66 because it said so on the front license plate. He went to the passenger door and pulled it open. The etiquette took her by surprise.

"Um, thanks," she said, slipping into the car.

She watched him walk around the front of the vehicle. Their eyes met through the windshield.

"What am I doing here?" she whispered through clenched teeth. "None of this makes sense. Who are you, Rory MacGregor?"

## Chapter Five

Rory knew this wasn't a date. It was drive-thru coffee suggested by his sister with the woman who had tried to kill him the night before with an ancient blade.

Still, he felt his heart beating a little faster when he looked at her. His magick tingled beneath his flesh, filling him with awareness. He wanted to be here, next to her, with her.

There was also a sense of danger.

Rory needed to believe the look in her eyes when she gazed at him with a cross between confusion and innocence. How could this be the same woman who'd tried to attack him? Maybe she'd been possessed by a wood spirit? Or perhaps someone had cursed the blade she found. Stranger things had happened in Green Vallis. He didn't want to consider that behind her beautiful brown eyes lurked something darker.

Though they had not lived there long, it was clear that Green Vallis was a special place. All of the MacGregors had felt it the second they drove into the city limits. A convergence of ley lines beneath the surface created a powerful vortex that fed their magick. Like all things, magick needed fuel to work. Normally that energy came from nature, which had been difficult in their previous home.

New York City had a lot of metal and concrete, and very little by way of plant life. What it did have was large crowds, which made it easy to hide in plain sight. No one really paid attention to a man walking around in a kilt, and foreign accents didn't tend to stick out as they did in their current Midwestern home.

Although the family had thrived in many ways in the city, their magick had starved. They could only take so much power-infusing life from Central Park and community gardens before they killed every plant in Manhattan like a magickal plague.

In contrast, the mansion his extended family had purchased in Green Vallis came with eighty acres of forest. Here, they could take the energy they needed from the woods as a whole without killing a single tree. There was more than enough to keep their magick healthy. They could live at peace with nature, taking care of it as it took care of them.

He glanced at Jennifer, letting his gaze slide down to her legs to where she clutched her apron. There was another way to fuel magick, one they'd had to resort to quite often in New York City— sex. Sexual energy could give a quick infusion, much like a rush of adrenaline. It wasn't sustainable and didn't last all that long, but damn, it was fun.

Unfortunately, Green Vallis's power also attracted unsavory supernatural creatures. The ley lines pulsed like a beacon, welcoming good and evil without discrimination. In the few short years they had lived there, they'd fought a psychic entity called a *lidérc*, numerous ghosts, gremians, trolls, goblins, leprechauns, a banshee, possessions, demon spawns, and a couple of regular sick-ass murdering humans.

There were even a few non-threatening supernaturals living in town, like Jefferson, Jennifer's boss. He was a third-generation dhampir, the product of a vampire and human pairing. The family was keeping an eye on him. The last thing they wanted was vampires coming to town, but the man didn't appear connected to a den.

Despite all these inconveniences, the MacGregor family was determined to make it work. They were not giving up Green Vallis without a fight. And they sure as hell weren't leaving it to become overrun by those with malevolent intent.

"This is awkward, huh?" Jennifer said, breaking the silence.

"Excuse me?"

"You didn't have to agree to give me a ride. I know you are being polite because Maura suggested it," she said. "After taking me to the motel last night and making sure I was unharmed, you've done more than enough. I'm fine if you want to take me straight to the Crimson Tavern. Or here. I can get out here and walk."

Rory realized he hadn't been talking. His mind had been drifting. He needed to figure out the question of who this woman was and what had happened the night before.

"Who have ya been around, love, that such an idea is even a remote possibility?" Rory demanded, unable to help himself. "Who would drop a woman in the middle of town, blocks away from her destination? And before fulfilling the simple promise of coffee?"

She leaned slightly away from him, her eyes focusing on his face.

"I only meant to say it's not a very gentle-manly thing to do." He eased his tone as he tried to explain.

"All right," she said. Her hands had tightened on the apron.

"Any man worth the name would help a woman in distress," he insisted.

"All right," she repeated.

"I said I'd give ya ride, and I meant it," he continued.

"Thanks," she answered, her tone a little flat. "The ride is appreciated."

She looked like he'd been yelling at her. So much for his MacGregor charm. What the hell was wrong with him? He should be compli-menting her and making her laugh, not lecturing her about whatever it was he was lecturing her about.

"All I meant was—"

"I get it," she interrupted. "It wasn't my inten-tion to insult your manhood."

"I don't think ya insulted my manhood."

"Your gentlemanly-hood then."

"I don't think ya insulted me."

"All right."

He wished she'd stop saying that. It made him feel like a little kid being tolerated by a tired parent.

"Ya don't remember anything from the forest last night?" He twisted his hands against the steering wheel.

Since moving to Green Vallis, all of his cousins who'd been born of Uncle Angus and Aunt Margareta had found their true loves—Erik found Lydia, Iain found Jane, Euann found Cora, Malina re-found her luck demon Dar, Niall found Charlotte, and Kenneth found Andrea. Even Uncle Fergus had found the reincarnation of his long-dead wife, Elspeth.

The odds of meeting a *fíorghrá*, a true love, were astronomical, considering they lived for hundreds of years. But for so many of his clan to have met them here, now? It was almost too much to comprehend. It had to be part of the local magick, or so Rory hoped.

For some stupid reason, he'd convinced himself Jennifer was going to mean something special to him. The second that he saw her he'd felt his world change.

Maybe after seven pairings for the MacGregor family, fate thought it had done enough.

Rory couldn't help but be jealous. He had no problem finding women to have sex with him, but he wanted more. He wanted a connection, a wife, someone who loved him unconditionally, and who he could love in return with every fiber of his being.

In searching for that dream, that wish, he was afraid he'd start desperately trying to force any women he met into that mold. Was that what happened with Jennifer? Was he taking the fact she'd tried to murder him and twisting it into some sign that wasn't there?

"Any of these will work," Jennifer said, glancing out the window to direct his attention to the fast food places he drove past.

The idea of taking her through a fast food drive-thru for a coffee left him a little sick to his stomach. They probably brewed it next to the fryers, and it would taste like French fry grease. This was not how a man treated a lady the first time they went somewhere together. His ma would lock him in his room for a month if she found out. Sure, he was hundreds of years old and a man, but warlocks still knew not to cross their elders.

However, since this wasn't a date and he was already failing miserably at conversation, Rory turned into the next restaurant. He pulled into line behind a minivan. Someone had affixed stickers of a mom, dad, and three children to the back window. The normality of it made him jealous.

Jennifer dug into her apron. "Can you order

me a number two with a large coffee and cream, please?"

She pulled her hand from her apron and tried to give him money to pay for it.

"I got this," he said.

"No, it's—"

"I insist," he cut her off.

"Thank you." Jennifer sighed and looked out the passenger window. She clutched her money in her hand.

The car again fell into silence. He made his way through the drive-thru, talking only to order her number two and a couple of coffees. After he received their order, he handed the bag of food to her.

"Thanks." Jennifer was careful not to touch his hand when she took the food from him. She didn't open it to check the contents as she placed it on her lap with the apron.

Rory took an obligatory sip of the hot coffee and hid his grimace. Just as he expected, the bitter flavor had the underlying taste of a deep-fat fryer.

"Which way?" he asked, coming to a stop sign.

"You can drop me off at the Crimson Tavern. I'll make my way from there." Jennifer fingered the plastic lid on her cup, tapping a light rhythm on the top.

"I can take ya home." Rory wanted to be a gentleman, but she made it damn hard.

"I…" The tapping stopped.

Rory inhaled a deep breath and slowly nodded, understanding her hesitance. "You're worried about me seeing where ya live? 'Cause I'm a stranger?"

Jennifer nodded.

"If it makes ya feel any better, this is a small town. I can probably figure it out by asking around. I'm pretty sure Mrs. Callister, the local busybody, keeps a record of everyone." He smiled, hoping to make her at least chuckle once on this drive.

"You've seen it?" Jennifer grimaced. "What she says about Kay and me is a lie. We just waitress. We're not prostitutes. Honestly, my job is hard enough without her blog posts making guys think they can get lucky in the back room between appetizers and the main course for ten bucks. If you think I'm going to blow you for a couple of bucks, you're mistaken."

Rory's hand tightened on the coffee cup and the lid popped off, spilling hot liquid on his hand and leg. "Ow, damn it!"

The car swerved before he managed to apply the brakes a little too hard.

"Oh!" Jennifer braced a hand on the dashboard and lifted her cup in the air to keep it from sloshing around.

Luckily, the coffee mainly landed on his kilt and not the bare legs underneath, even though he could feel the heat of it against his crotch.

"Oh, ouch," Jennifer acknowledged as she set her cup on the floor and dug into her food bag to pull out napkins. She handed them over. "Did it burn?"

"I'll be fine." He took the napkins and blotted the kilt. "Though I can't say the same for Mrs. Callister. That nuisance has to be stopped. By calling respectable women whores, she's gone too far this time."

"More inferred," Jennifer said as if trying to downplay the seriousness.

"And I never thought that about ya," he said.

"She's said worse about others. She tried to imply my boss is in witness protection from the mafia and running drugs out of the back room. I don't think anyone believes her. I actually kind of feel sorry for her. She must be lacking something inside to feel the need to lie about her neighbors like she does."

"That's very understanding of ya," he said. "Still, something needs to be done."

A car passed, and she stared at the driver through the window, turning her head to watch the vehicle. "Turn toward the Crimson Tavern, then keep going. My place is pretty much a straight shot from there," she said.

Rory smiled to himself. She might be relaxing around him. Though he couldn't fault her for being cautious. Women living on their own needed to take extra precautions. He had to remind himself that humans were not like warlocks. As a human, she would have been very shaken at having woken up in a motel with no idea of how she arrived there. In contrast, when Rory woke up tied to a tree with no memory of his abduction, he had felt like it was another family prank.

Whoever had bespelled her might try again. He needed to protect her.

He turned the corner and drove past the tavern. "Maybe ya should stay at my family home for a while or the motel if you're more comfortable."

"That's a..." She frowned, studying him. "Either a very inappropriately strange or a very kind offer. Either way, no thank you. I have a home."

"I don't seem to be articulating myself very well this morning." He gave a small laugh. "Maybe I shouldn't have spilled that coffee since it sounds like I need it. What I meant to say is, if ya don't remember what happened, it might be a case of better safe than sorry. My sister won't charge ya for the room. I can drive ya back there after ya pick up some of your belongings if ya like."

"I appreciate the kind offer, but I'll be fine," she said. "You can stop here."

Rory pulled over to the curb. There were several houses in the neighborhood.

Jennifer opened the car door and put one foot outside the door. "Thank you for the ride and for helping me out last night. If you're ever at Crimson Tavern, I'll buy you a plate of nachos." She got out of the car and shut the door.

Rory watched as she went to the sidewalk. He was going to make sure she got home safely, but she stood staring at him. She lifted her hand in a small wave, and it became clear she wasn't going home until he left.

With a sigh, Rory gave a small wave of his fingers and obliged. He pulled away from the curb and watched her through his rearview mirror. She didn't move as she waited for him to turn out of sight.

"I will be seeing ya again, lassie," Rory whispered. "That is a promise."

# Chapter Six

Jennifer popped the lid off her coffee and took a long drink. It was more for the caffeine than the taste. Half was gone when she finished, and she put the lid back on for the walk home. She was about a block away from her trailer. Since she didn't want Rory following her there, she waited another minute to make sure he didn't turn back.

There was nothing wrong with where she lived. Sure, it wasn't a mansion on a hill overlooking town like royalty over its flock, but it was hers for now. She paid her rent, kept it clean, and when she was inside, she was safe from the outside world.

Even now, Jennifer felt the simmering anger that surfaced when she was near him. In the car, it had become difficult to concentrate on anything else. She had done her best to be polite, if not nice to him when she had really wanted to throw her hot coffee in his face.

Jennifer felt terrible for her unwarranted feelings. Violence was not in her nature. That rage was reason enough to stay away from him.

"If you're ever at Crimson Tavern, I'll buy you a plate of nachos," she mocked herself under her breath. Why the hell didn't she say thank you and leave it at that? She couldn't see him again—not with her irrational temper.

Had he done something to her, and was this her body's way of reminding her of an event she couldn't remember? It didn't feel like that was the case, but then, she'd been unconscious. How could she know?

She cut between two houses to where the trailer home was parked near an alleyway. The light blue paint covering the bottom half of the unit was chipped and dirty. Someone had painted the top half white much more recently. Lattice covered the bottom edge of the trailer to hide the fact cinderblocks supported it. Bowed stairs led to a windowless front door. A pair of double doors were a few feet away from it, but they had been bolted shut long ago and no longer provided a way in or out of her bedroom.

Jennifer reached into the front of her shirt and

pulled a chain from around her neck. It held her house key. She glanced around before unlocking the door. Inside, brown carpet and beige walls created a bland palette. A blue couch had been there when she'd moved in. The middle cushion sank lower than the two that flanked it. The small television didn't get reception, but the built-in VCR worked. She could watch movies from the 1980s collection someone had left behind in the bedroom closet.

One picture hung on the living room wall of Jennifer with her father and brother. Presumably, her mother had taken it.

"Hi, guys. How was your night?" she asked the photo. "Mine was…"

She let her words trail off with a deep sigh. Somehow talking to ghosts seemed too sad this morning.

The living room led to a small kitchen. Jennifer put her coffee cup on the counter and emptied her apron next to it. Then she dug into the food bag. They had messed up her order, but in the end, it didn't matter if it was a sausage biscuit or a bacon one. It was food in her stomach.

She ate the biscuit on her way down the hall, holding it in her mouth as she stripped out of her smelly clothes. A portable washing machine used for camping was outside her bathroom door. A water hose was hooked up to the bathroom faucet, and the drain hose disappeared into a hole in the floor, filled with caulk. It made it impossible to close the bathroom door, but it hardly mattered since she lived alone. Shoving her work clothes and apron into it, she started a fast-clean cycle.

Her clean uniform had dried on the shower rod, and she pulled the items down before starting the shower. The routine was automatic, and she had shampoo in her hair before she'd even thought about what she was doing.

Today felt lonelier than most. It started as an ache in her chest, squeezing her throat. She closed her eyes and let the water hit her face to hide any tears that might try to fall.

Seeing Maura, Rory, and Bruce had reminded her what it had been like to have a family. Their closeness was evident in the way they teased each other. The anger she'd felt faded. Rory seemed like a nice guy. He'd given her a ride, bought her breakfast, didn't leave her unconscious in a forest. All of those were very nice-guy things.

Then why the rage?

It made no sense.

*"There you are."*

The gravelly voice sounded like it came from outside the shower. Jennifer gasped, nearly falling as she whipped the shower curtain open, ready to fight. "Who's there?"

She fumbled for a weapon, only finding a shampoo bottle. She held it like a club.

"What are you doing in my house?" she demanded.

About right now, she regretted not taking a phone with her everywhere.

"I'm calling the cops. They'll be here any moment," she lied.

Jennifer didn't hear anything but running water. She swatted at the handle, keeping an eye on the open bathroom door. The water blasted her with cold before she finally managed to turn it off.

Shaking, she stepped out of the shower, still wielding the half-empty bottle. Water dripped from her body onto the floor. It ran from her hair into her eyes.

The washing machine made a clunking noise as it agitated the load. Jennifer tried to listen past it for movement. Slowly, she grabbed a towel and used it to wipe the water from her face.

She hadn't imagined it. Someone had spoken.

Had she scared them off?

Were they waiting in the hallway?

Her hands shook as she dried herself, still gripping the shampoo bottle. She dropped the towel on the floor and quickly pulled the shirt over her head.

"The cops are coming," she yelled. "You better be gone."

*Thump. Thump. Thump.*

The portable washer kept spinning.

She crept to the bathroom door and slowly looked out, ready to strike as she glanced in both directions. No one was there.

Jennifer grabbed her clean clothes and held them against her stomach. She took a deep, terrified breath as she rushed toward escape. Gazing into the living room, she half-expected someone to jump out at her. It was empty.

Her shoulder slammed into the front door, but it didn't open.

She made a weak noise, something between a moan and a scream as she hit it again. It took several attempts before her fingers managed to pull the handle. The door swung open, and she tripped down the stairs.

Air hit her damp, naked lower half as she looked around the area. No one was outside, and the open space gave her comfort. The alley rarely had traffic, and the surrounding houses with their old fences provided a little bit of privacy. She dropped her clothes on the grass-patched dirt that doubled as a yard.

Jennifer fumbled as she tried to quickly dress, pulling on her panties and black slacks for work. She kept glancing around the area to be sure nobody watched her. The door to her trailer home hung open. She pulled her arms inside her shirt and kept it on so that she could thread her arms into her bra while maintaining minimal privacy.

Jennifer stared at the trailer, watching for the curtains to move, for a sign that someone was in there. She found comfort in being dressed as she pulled on her socks and shoes, doing her best to brush the dirt from her feet. Her wet hair dampened her shoulders and back.

She wasn't crazy. She *had* heard a voice.

Part of her wanted to run.

Part of her knew she should look inside.

Another part told her to call the police, which was difficult without a phone. Where had she put hers anyway? Probably uncharged in a drawer somewhere. She could rouse a neighbor and ask to borrow one, but then it would become a big ordeal.

"Fuck," she muttered to herself, picking her apron off the ground. She thought of Rory's offer to stay at the motel and wished she had taken it.

Jennifer crept toward the open door, still debating on what to do. The steady thump of the washer came from within. Without taking the stairs to go inside, she reached to shut the door. It remained unlocked, but aside from the meager tips sitting on her counter from the night before, there was nothing to steal.

Jennifer tried to peek around the curtains hanging over the bolted double doors to her bedroom. From what little she saw, no one moved inside.

A feeling of dread crept its way along her spine. She couldn't force herself to go back inside.

Jennifer stepped backward, moving to the path between the two houses that led to the street. Only when the trailer was out of sight did she turn around. She ran to the sidewalk and hurried toward work. Never had she been so thankful for a double shift in all her life.

## Chapter Seven

"Aye, we found a bog wench in the forest." Raibeart's voice drifted from the dining room.

Rory frowned and paused on his way up the stairs to listen. What was his uncle doing now?

Rory studied his hand against the oak banister. It looked brand-new, even though it had been splintered when their home was invaded by a run of bad luck—fairies, ghosts, demons, and goblins. With sixty-plus rooms in the mansion, the restoration had taken their collective magick to repair all the damage the infestation had done.

"She tried to kill Rory, but I'm not holding that against her," Raibeart continued. "She wouldn't be the first lassie to take offense to him, and I daresay she'll not be the last."

"Raibeart, what nonsense are ya talking

now?" Rory grumbled to himself. He turned to look toward the marble floor below, watching to see who might come out of the dining room. No one did.

There was something very special about this home, unlike the others they'd had in the past. Being inside the walls made him feel powerful. The house was always full. MacGregors were always coming and going. Like Rory, some lived in the home full time, while others—like his cousins Iain, Erik, and Niall—lived close enough to be available but far enough that the rest of them couldn't monitor them. Well, that wasn't entirely true. Niall and his wife, Charlotte, had an apartment in town but were currently traveling the United States in an RV.

Upstairs were mainly bedrooms and then access to the roof. Downstairs was the main foyer, dining room, and library. Beyond the dining room was the kitchen, offices, and an entire back wing sprawled out with more bedrooms than he cared to count and access to the back gardens.

"I think this one might be the one," Raibeart said.

"The one what?" his ma's voice asked.

"The one I ask to marry me," Raibeart answered.

"A bog witch?" his ma insisted. "Ya want to bring a bog witch into the family?"

Rory sighed and started back down the stairs to defend Jennifer's honor before Raibeart accidentally tarnished it.

"Fly, Uncle Chicken!" The youngest MacGregor's shout caused Rory to whip around to face the open balcony of the second level. Jewel had more power than all of them combined bundled into her little body. She inherited phoenix magick from her mother. The woman had died in ritualistic childbirth, leaving Jewel to be raised by her father, Kenneth. Very long, long, *loooong* story short, Jewel kidnapped a woman named Andrea. Kenneth fell in love with Andrea, and the two were now married. Andrea also inherited the power to contain Jewel's magick...which apparently wasn't working at the moment.

Iain came flying from the top balcony in his bird-shifter form, followed by bursts of rainbows and bubbles. All of Angus and Margareta's sons had the ability to shift. That MacGregor line had been tainted by a spell, or at least that was Rory's best guess. The problem with Iain was, once he shifted, he tended not to want to come out of it.

"Pretty Uncle Chicken!" Jewel tried to climb onto the railing to jump from the second floor.

Rory didn't move, not wanting the girl to

notice him. It wasn't that he didn't love the five-year-old, but Jewel was one scary kid when she was in play mode. One of the last times she'd "played" with him, he'd ended up with a painfully tight ballerina bun and a shimmering tutu. His natural athletic abilities leaned toward golf and shinty, not pirouettes and leaping across the floor. That was actually the reason he'd cut his hair.

Of course, that had been in Jewel's previous life. As a phoenix, her powers came with one very ugly catch. Without Andrea to temper it back, the child would flame out to be reborn. The family hoped that this time she would last into adulthood.

"Sorry!" Andrea came running out of one of the bedrooms in a bathrobe. She snagged Jewel around the waist before she could leap after Iain. Since he was the only one in the front room, she gave Rory an apologetic look. "I thought she was sleeping. I took the binding bracelet off just long enough to take a shower."

Still holding Jewel, she pulled a bracelet out of her pocket and slipped it onto her wrist. Jewel's eyes flashed, and Andrea placed her on the floor.

The rainbows and bubbles stopped. Iain circled the foyer before coming close to the floor. He shifted and landed on his feet.

"Is everything all right?" Margareta called from the dining room entryway.

"Yep, got her," Andrea yelled, leading Jewel back toward the bedrooms.

"Iain, when did ya get here?" Margareta asked. She was a petite woman but mighty. Anyone who knew her knew not to cross her.

"Hey, Ma." Iain went to his mother to kiss her on the cheek. He acted as if nothing had happened. Considering the MacGregor household always seemed to be in a state of chaos, his attitude wasn't surprising. "Just came by to grab my formal kilt. Taking Jane out tonight. It's a surprise, so don't tell her."

"Family dinner Sunday," Margareta said.

"We'll be here." Iain took the stairs two at a time. "Hey, Rory. I see you're back. Heard ya were being sexed up by a bog witch. Can't say I blame ya for trying to hide your slumming from the family."

"What?" Rory frowned. "That's not—"

"Methinks my lady doth protest too much," Iain teased with a laugh as he disappeared down the hall. His muffled voice shouted, "Ya should bring her to Sunday dinner. We'll put plastic down on her seat, so she doesn't muddy up the nice furniture."

"Don't ya dare, laddie," Margareta scolded.

"I'll not have a bog witch at my table. It's bad enough Kenneth brought those mountain witches into our lives."

Rory turned to his aunt and ignored the comment about Kenneth. "Jennifer is not a bog witch. She's just a woman who needed help."

"A woman you're dating?" At that, Margareta smiled and stepped fully into the foyer. "Perhaps ya should bring her dinner. Let us get a look at her."

"Don't give me that look," Rory admonished, keeping his tone playful. "Just because ya got all of your children married off doesn't mean it's my turn."

He smiled as he said it, but secretly the words stung. Jealousy filled him each time he saw the happy newlyweds together. He wanted what they had. He wanted a wife he could spoil with surprise dates. He wanted to hear his name whispered in the night, knowing that it came from a place of intense love.

But he didn't want to enchant just any woman. He wanted the love to be real. After hundreds of years, he was more than ready to take that step. Until Green Vallis, he had never really dared to hope it might happen, but the town was special.

"Wench, not witch," Raibeart said from behind Margareta.

"She's just a nice lady who needed our assistance," Rory corrected. He finished coming down the stairs to join his family in the dining room.

"The only lady who needed help was tied to a tree," Raibeart said.

"What lady? There were two?" Murdoch, Rory's da asked. Like all the MacGregor men, he had dark hair and proud features. People say Rory and Bruce favored him.

Rory saw his parents sitting across from each at the long wooden table. A fancy cake sat between them with a slice missing. The crooked lines of frosting decoration gave away that this was another of his ma's attempts at baking like a human with no magickal help. The attempts were rarely good.

Actually, they were never good.

"Me," Rory said dryly so Raibeart wouldn't answer for him. "I'm the lady in this story."

Murdoch laughed and nodded. "Been there, my boy."

"While we're on the subject," Raibeart interjected. "Did a package come for me today? I'm expecting something important."

"No," Margareta answered.

"Rory, ya know I don't like it when ya take off like that," Cait, his ma, scolded, pushing up from her seat. She looked the part of the stereotypical 1950s housewife but looks could be deceiving. She had a fondness for cashmere sweaters, pearls, and something she called the circle skirt. She kept her blonde-brown hair neatly pulled back. "Next time, leave a note."

"I didn't have a choice." Rory didn't want to get into this. His ma and aunt would only worry, and his da and uncles would tease him mercilessly. "Some force abducted me out of the shower. I woke up in the forest tied naked to a tree with enchanted rope."

"Which one of my sons did it this time?" Margareta MacGregor's voice was low and soft, a sure sign she was annoyed. "God knows I love ya boys, but ya are all idiots."

"And I saved him!" Raibeart announced over her. "I also got me a fine knife."

Raibeart pulled the scian from a scabbard on his waist to show them the ancient blade.

"Let me see that," Cait ordered, waving her hand to call the blade out of Raibeart's grip with magick. It flew through the air at her head, but she caught it with ease. She furrowed her brow. "Who had this?"

"It's mine," Raibeart said. He waved his fingers to call the blade back. The knife flew out of Cait's hand. Raibeart caught it. "Finders keepers I got peepers."

"It's cursed," Cait corrected. "I feel a strange magickal vibration coming from it."

"That's nothing. Just a wee twitch." Raibeart tried to put it back in his scabbard.

Cait used her magick to force the blade out of the scabbard. It again flew across the room. She caught it as it neared her. "No. I think we need to put it in the—"

"Mine," Raibeart said, trying to take the knife back. The blade turned, flying toward him.

"Raibeart," Cait scolded, waving her hand again.

The knife flew back and forth as they fought over it.

Suddenly, it headed off course, targeting Rory.

Rory lifted his arms to block his face and ducked.

"Watch it," Murdoch yelled when it came too close to hitting his son. He waved his hand upward. His magick forced the blade to shoot up and embed itself into the ceiling.

"Ya know the rule, Raibeart. Cursed objects go in the vault," Margareta said.

"Ya always take away my toys," Raibeart pouted. His kilt shimmered to be replaced by a black leotard and pink tutu. "I'm going to go where I'm appreciated. Jewel and I have dance lessons."

Glitter sprinkled from him as he marched from the dining room.

"There is something seriously wrong with that man," Margareta said with a dismissing laugh.

"Rory, come here and try your ma's cake." Murdoch suppressed a grin as he lifted the slice in front of him.

"I had breakfast—" Rory tried to excuse himself.

"Nonsense," Murdoch interrupted. "Take mine."

Rory knew he wasn't getting out of it as he walked around the table to sit by his father. "Thanks, Da." He took the plate with the uneaten slice on it. "Ma, this looks amazing. Would ya mind giving Da another piece? I don't feel right taking this one from him."

Murdoch kicked him under the table. Rory gave a small cough.

Cait handed her husband another slice.

"Thank ya, my love." Murdoch gazed lovingly at her. All his life, Rory had seen his father look at his mother just like that. And, knowing his da, he would eat every single bite of that cake no matter how bad it tasted, just to make her smile.

That is what Rory wanted. He wanted that kind of love.

He thought of Jennifer. The conversation between them had been stunted and awkward, and then there was the whole she-had-tried-to-stab-him thing. Logic told him to stay away and to tell his family there was danger.

He couldn't form the words.

"You're not eating," his ma noted.

"Oh, uh…" Rory automatically looked at his father's plate to see if he'd taken a bite first. Murdoch seemed to be waiting on him to go first.

"Is this bog witch thing something to worry about?" Cait furrowed her brow.

Rory knew that look. It instantly made him want to confess everything like a little kid in trouble.

"Raibeart was telling the truth this time, wasn't he?" Cait crossed her arms over her chest.

"I don't know what it is," Rory said. "And her name is Jennifer, not Bog Witch."

"Jennifer what?" Cait asked.

"I don't know. Just Jennifer," he answered.

"Ya mean there really was danger?" Margareta leaned closer to Cait to add her motherly stare to the equation as both women tried to force a confession out of him.

Rory picked up a fork and cut into the cake.

He lifted a bite and mumbled, "I'm not sure," before placing it in his mouth. Salt exploded over his taste buds, and he fought to keep from spitting it out. He put his fork on the table.

"Well?" his ma asked.

"Mm." He tried to nod.

"Let me try—" Murdoch began, reaching for a fork.

Rory put his hand on his da's to stop him. He couldn't swallow. Standing, he grabbed a napkin from a stack that had been set out and spat his bite into is as artfully as he could.

Cait frowned.

"Ma did ya happen to mix up salt and sugar again?" he asked, wishing a drink was nearby.

Murdoch dropped his fork.

"No, did I?" Cait picked up the slice and brought a tiny bit to her lips. She made a face and shook her head. "Oh, that's not good at all." She grabbed the cake to carry it back to the kitchen with a dejected look on her face. They could hear her throwing it in the trash.

"Owe ya one, son," his da whispered.

Rory kept the napkin to his lips and tried to spit more of the salty taste out of his mouth.

"I give up." Cait walked back in empty-handed. She wiggled her fingers. Sparkles of magick rained over the table, and a new cake appeared where the old one had been. This one was decorated to magazine-cover perfection and was about three times as big as the first. "I don't get it. I can boil a potion with my eyes closed, but this…" She waved her hand in frustration.

"My love, ya have so many skills, leave human cooking to the mortals," Murdoch told his wife. "Let them have this one thing."

"Rory don't think ya are getting out of answering," Margareta said. "What happened?"

He made a move to stand from the table. His ma held up her hand. Yellow light swirled around her fingertips in warning.

Rory settled back into his chair. "I was taking a shower, and the next thing I know I was tied to a tree with enchanted ropes, and I couldn't use my magick to escape."

"Sounds like your cousins," Cait said.

"Aye," Margareta and Murdoch agreed in unison.

"Uncle Raibeart found me on one of his midnight runs, and I convinced him to free me." Rory tried to stand again. Cait lifted a finger and pointed that he should remain seated.

"Continue," Cait said. "Where did the knife come from?"

"Jennifer was there chasing a lost puppy," Rory said. "I thought she'd found it, but instead, she discovered the cursed knife. Until that moment, she couldn't see me or the enchanted rope. Raibeart stopped her from coming after me, but he stunned her pretty good with an energy ball. We had to take her to the motel to sleep it off."

"I have to ask, son," Murdoch said. "Did ya drink anything with Raibeart before all this happened? Because it seems a little…"

"Strange," Cait finished.

"Aye," Aunt Margareta agreed.

"Are ya seeing little fairies dancing around your head?" his da continued.

"It happened," Rory assured them. "I need to go check on Jennifer and make sure everything is all right with her. She didn't remember any of it, but since this was a supernatural event and she's human, we owe it to her to make sure she's unharmed."

"So you're sure she's not a bog witch?" Cait asked.

"She's not a bog anything. She's just a pretty girl who was in the wrong place at the wrong time," Rory said, instantly regretting his words.

"Pretty?" Cait perked up a little.

"I mean, yeah, for a human." Rory tried to downplay the comment.

"Do ya think…?" Cait looked at Margareta.

"I don't see why not," Margareta answered.

"Before ya start planning my wedding, maybe ya could see to it that the cursed knife is put away somewhere safe?" Rory stood and pointed toward the ceiling.

The blade was gone with only a hole to show for it.

"Raibeart," Margareta muttered, leaving to confront the man.

"I think he kept the enchanted rope, too," Rory called after her as she stormed from the room to collect the scian. "Might want to get that from him."

"Ya are unharmed?" His ma leaned forward to grab his hands, now that he was alone in the dining room with his parents.

"I'm fine, Ma, I promise," Rory said.

"And the puppy?" his da asked. "Did ya find the puppy?"

Rory smiled and nodded. All of the MacGregors were animal lovers. "Aye. The puppy is safe. The motel staff is spoiling him. I was actually thinking of keeping him. He's a cute little guy. Traitor could use a playmate, I think. They say it keeps the older dogs young to have a puppy around."

Traitor was his uncle Fergus's English bulldog.

"I'm sure Fergus will help ya with the enchantments when it comes time," Murdoch said. That was one benefit of being a warlock. Pets lived much longer than their expected lifespans. Fergus swore by enchantments and potions, but Rory always thought it had to do with the animals absorbing magick left over from their owners. The constant stream of it helped keep them young and healthy.

"So, pretty Jennifer?" his ma prompted as if being alone with his parents would make him more willing to talk about his love life.

"Ma, I don't know. I gave her a ride home, and she didn't seem interested in dating me. I'm more concerned with the cursed object that's trying to kill me." Rory patted her hand before standing from the table.

"I can tell ya like her," Cait said. "I know my son."

"Ya have to woo the ones who are worth it," Murdoch advised.

"Ya mean take a potion to turn myself into a bird and serenade her from outside her window as ya did in the olden days?" Rory teased. "She might think I'm Iain, and that would cause all kinds of problems between him and Jane."

"I hear they hold up boom boxes now for that," Cait offered.

"Who's been holding up your boom boxes?"

Murdoch pretended to be upset. Cait came around the table to kiss her husband.

"I'm out of here. This is about to get weird." Rory headed toward the door.

"Check in," Cait ordered. "Let us know you're all right, or we'll come looking for ya."

"She works at Crimson Tavern. I'll be there. Don't show up at her work. Ya might scare her off." Rory quickened his steps as he went toward the stairs.

"No magick is strong enough to hold Raibeart the Great!" Raibeart ran from the back rooms. Cloth fairy wings flapped with each step. Jewel's laughter followed him, as did Margareta's scolding.

"Raibeart!" Margareta yelled.

Rory took the steps two at a time and hurried to his bedroom. He shut the door on the chaos erupting behind him.

## Chapter Eight

Rory felt the breath rush out of him as his bedroom door shut behind him. He blinked—only to open his eyes to darkness. The door had not led to his bedroom. He tried to move but found his body wedged between a concrete wall and wooden planks. The room carried with it a musty odor, like stale air and bags of flour. A protrusion dug into his back.

"Not again," he whispered, trying to wriggle free. His magick refused to rise when he called it forth. He slammed his shoulder forward, trying to dislodge himself. The more he fought, the tighter the wood seemed to press him into place until each breath became painful.

This time it was impossible to dismiss what was happening as a prank.

"Hello?" his breath came out on a pant, and the sound was barely loud enough for *him* to hear, let alone anyone else.

Seconds ticked by, each one feeling like an eternity as he waited. And all he could do was wait—wait for the light, wait for someone to come, wait for the pressure on his chest to ease, or for it to press in so hard he died from asphyxiation.

Rory felt himself starting to panic. His hand began to tingle where the blood didn't flow.

A door pushed open, and light flooded the space before him. He eagerly looked to see where he was being held. The wooden planks were the ends of restaurant pantry shelves pressing him into a brick wall. Large cans of ketchup came into focus. He tilted his head to see past them.

"Straws, ranch dressing, coffee." Jennifer came through the door mumbling to herself.

Rory felt the panic leave. Seeing her calmed him, which he knew was ridiculous because she'd been enchanted to kill him the last time they were in a similar position.

Jennifer wore her work uniform. What looked to be a twist tie from a bread bag held her hair back from her face. He wondered at the odd choice in accessory. She reached for a light switch. "Straws, ranch dressing, cof—"

"Jennifer," Rory interrupted, the sound of her voice propelling him to force the words out. "I'm so glad to see ya. I—"

"I need straws, ranch dressing, coffee." Jennifer looked over the shelves, not hearing or seeing him. She lifted up on her toes to look at the top shelf. "Straws, ranch dressing, coffee."

"Jennifer," Rory repeated, grunting the word.

"Ah, straws. There you are." She reached her hand to the high shelf, feeling around where she couldn't see. He heard her fingers tapping on the wood. "Come…here…you…"

The sound of metal slid against the shelf. She dropped back on her heels and turned toward him. The cursed scian was back in her hand. Why wasn't it locked away in the vault?

Her eyes met his.

"There you are," she said.

"Jenn, wait." He leaned into the shelf, trying desperately to dislodge himself.

"There you are," she repeated, lifting the blade over her shoulder as she prepared to strike.

"Yo, hurry up. I need coffee like yesterday!" The door burst open, and another waitress entered the storage area.

Jennifer blinked in confusion and lowered her arm. Rory managed to push the shelf a couple of inches and slipped out from where it had him pinned. He snatched the blade from her hand.

"Whoa, hey," the waitress said with a teasing laugh. "I thought we agreed, no turning tricks in the back room."

"Kay?" Jennifer glanced between Kay and Rory. "What?"

"I should be the one asking you what," Kay quipped. "You do know it's rush hour, don't you?"

"My fault," Rory said. "I was trying to convince Jennifer to go out with me tonight after her shift."

Jennifer turned to him and whispered, "You were?"

Seeing her beautifully confused expression, he found he very much wanted a real date with her. There was something about her eyes that haunted him and made him want to lean closer.

"I must not have been doing a good job of it if ya don't remember." He forced a smile even though his chest still ached.

"She says yes," Kay answered for her as she went to grab coffee grounds from the shelf. "Girl, it's about time you when out. And if it's a rich, sexy MacGregor in a kilt, more power to you. Also, your table three needs soda refills. I don't have time to do everything."

Kay left the storage room.

"I…" Jennifer looked after Kay and then back at him. "What's going on? How did you get in here?"

"That question requires a long answer," he said. "I think it should wait until after your shift. When do ya get off?"

"Uh…" She glanced around, but there wasn't a clock. "Like three hours?"

Three hours? He remembered she was working a double shift, so that meant it was late in the day. Like the last occasion he'd woke up trapped, time had slipped past him faster than he'd realized. He was missing part of a day. At least, he hoped it was only one day.

"Perfect, I'll wait for ya," Rory said.

"Is that a knife?" She eyed his hand and backed away from him.

"Yes. I'll explain it later," he said. There was no way he was putting the blade down. How it ended up back in her possession was beyond him, but clearly, his elders didn't do a very good job of securing the cursed object.

"I don't think you should have weapons in here," she said.

When she turned to glance at the door, Rory waved his hand and whispered an enchantment spell to force her to ignore the concern. He hated using magick on her but thought it for the best considering the circumstances.

"I'm so confused," she said, more to herself than to him. "Why am I even in here?"

"Oh, that I can help with." Rory reached along the high shelf to fetch the box of straws that had been pushed toward the back. He handed them to her. "Straws, ranch dressing, and Kay already took the coffee."

She took the straws and stared at them as if she couldn't focus.

"Oh, and um, here." He reached down and pulled out a giant plastic tub labeled "Ranch Dressing" in bold red script. It was next to a box of "Real" mashed potato flakes.

"Thanks?" She slowly took the container and cradled it against her waist.

"I have to ask." Rory pointed at the potatoes. "Real potatoes in a box?"

"Restaurant trick. For when people ask if we have real mashed potatoes, we can say yes." She turned to walk out the door.

Rory held it open for her. The smell of fried food wafted past them.

On her way out of the storage room, she glanced up at him. "You shouldn't be back here. It's staff only. If Kay mentions it to my boss, I could get in trouble and I need this job."

"I'll be at the bar," he said, following her from the storage room. The loud murmur of restaurant conversation drifted down the short hallway. "In case ya need me."

"Don't you mean you'll need *me*? I'm the one working," she said.

He followed her into the public area of the restaurant. "Of course."

"I'll bring you a menu." She darted away from him with the dressing and straws, moving toward the wait station as if the sound of work reactivated her senses.

Rory frowned at the knife and slipped it through the wide leather belt on his kilt. If someone had cursed the knife, he didn't want to use his magick directly on the weapon to hide it. Who knew what kind of adverse reaction that would have? At least this way, he could keep an eye on it and magickally make sure no one noticed it.

The Crimson Tavern was probably one of his favorite places to dine in town, though he hadn't been there for months. There was something appealing about the Old English tavern feel. The wooden floors and tables looked as if they could have come from centuries past. That is if he didn't take into account the very modern beer taps, flat-screen televisions, and neon signs.

Rory pulled his cellphone out of his pocket and waved his hand over it to dial his father.

"Rory? Are ya calling me from upstairs?" Murdoch asked by way of an answer.

"No, Da, I'm at the Crimson Tavern," Rory said. He glanced around to see if anyone was watching him a little too closely. He recognized several of the locals, but no one who gave him a reason to worry.

"How…?" Murdoch mumbled something, and it sounded like he was talking to someone else. "We were coming up to find ya, laddie. We're having trouble locating that cursed knife."

Rory looked down at the blade he still held. "I have it."

"He has it," Murdoch said.

Rory went to an empty place at the bar and lifted his hand, spreading his fingers wide to indicate a short glass. He mouthed "whiskey" to the bartender.

"Why does he have it?" His ma's voice came over the line. She must have been standing by her husband.

"Why did ya take the knife?" Murdoch repeated.

The bartender gestured toward at a bottle. Rory shook his head. The man pointed at a bottle higher on the shelf. Rory nodded. Into the phone, he said, "I didn't."

"But ya said ya took it." His da sighed. "Did ya or didn't ya take the cursed knife with ya?"

"I'm trying to explain."

"I'm listening," Murdoch stated.

Rory switched to Scottish Gaelic so his parents could understand him, but no one eavesdropping would. "When I stepped into my bedroom, I was transported to the Crimson Tavern and trapped in the storage room." Rory had to pause in his explanation while his father repeated his words to his mother. "The knife came with me."

The bartender slid a glass in front of him. He instantly took a long drink and enjoyed the familiar burn down his throat.

"Are ya sure ya haven't been drinking anything with Raibeart?" Cait insisted.

"No, Ma." Rory took another drink. He glanced around, making sure no one was watching him. The blade hadn't cursed itself.

"He says no," Murdoch repeated.

"I promised I'd call to check in, and I'm calling," Rory said, not giving his father time to ask more questions. "Tell Ma I'm fine. I'm going to wait for Jennifer to get off her shift, and then I'm taking her somewhere safe so we can figure out what's going on. I don't want to disrupt her life more than I have to, and we're not going to pull a Charlotte on her if she sees too much."

Charlotte was an unfortunate example of what happened when they had to erase too many memories from a human. In the end, it had been a miracle that she'd survived the madness. Most humans were not so lucky.

"Bring her here," Murdoch said.

"Oh, aye, good. We want to meet her," Cait said.

"I was thinking the motel," Rory replied, denying the request. He didn't want to bring Jennifer into the full force of the MacGregor household.

"What did he say?" Cait demanded.

"Motel," Murdoch answered.

"Tell him here is safer," Cait said. "I want to meet her."

"Your ma insists that here is safer," Murdoch said.

"I'll think about it," Rory answered. "I have to go, Da."

He hung up before they could say more.

A young girl came running by wielding a long French fry like a sword. She appeared to be a little younger than Jewel. Her brown eyes landed on his knife, and she grinned with the kind of fearless excitement only a child could express.

Rory dropped his arm over the blade to hide it from her. "I like yours better, little love." He nodded at her fry sword. The girl giggled.

"Beatrix, get back here." The girl's mother came to grab Beatrix's arm. The woman glanced at him and mumbled something like "sorry" before pulling the child back to their table.

Rory sipped the whiskey and watched Jennifer carrying a tray of sodas to one of her tables. Each one of her movements mesmerized him. Even without the cursed blade, she was a mystery he wanted to solve.

"Don't bother," the bartender said.

Rory turned to him in surprise.

"Many men have tried, and she's shot them all down," he said. "Jennifer's not that kind of girl."

Rory grinned. As a man, he liked the idea of a challenge. He held up his glass. "I'm going to need another one of these."

# Chapter Nine

Jennifer would have never thought she'd be happy to see a crazy man with a knife in the storage pantry. Rory MacGregor was a strange one, to be sure, but anything was better than going home to a possible intruder camping out in her home. She'd been worried about what she was going to do about that all night. The trailer no longer felt safe.

That voice had been real. Jennifer had heard it, felt it in her core. The fear lingered, and she was glad for the crowded restaurant.

It was almost worse that she hadn't seen an attacker. Her mind kept trying to convince her that it had been a ghost or something.

Yeah, right, ghost. What was next? Witches and werewolves?

"I'm losing it," she mumbled, staring at her order pad.

"Excuse me?" a lady with bouffant red hair and too much make up asked.

"I'll be right back with your drink. Margarita, classic lime, no salt," Jennifer answered the customer. She usually could remember orders without writing them down, but tonight her mind was scattered, and she was scribbling notes to keep afloat.

"And cheese fries," the woman added. She'd done the ordering, even for her husband. The woman clearly ruled her home with an iron fist because the man seemed afraid to look at any other female for too long.

"And cheese fries," Jennifer repeated, writing it down.

"Extra ranch," the woman said.

Jennifer nodded. "Extra ranch."

She felt Rory's eyes on her, or maybe she imagined it. He waited at the bar for his menu. She found she liked knowing he was there, watching out for her. Then there was the unreasonable rage-filled part of her that wanted to throw something at him.

What was he protecting her from?

How had he gotten into the storage room? She

barely remembered walking in there, let alone his asking to see her after work.

What the hell was happening to her? Her mind was flustered, and she couldn't concentrate. She felt like people were staring at her. Could she blame them? She was a freaking hot mess, thinking of ghosts and witches and home intruders. She needed this job, so there was no choice but to keep working. Running and hiding was not an option.

The very sexy Rory MacGregor oozed masculinity. He made her want to stab him and kiss him at the same time. The seed of rage was still there inside her, lingering, ready to flare up. But weren't anger and fierce passion close emotional cousins?

The redhead stared at her. Jennifer realized the woman was done and hurried to go.

Crap, what had the woman asked for?

Jennifer looked at her notepad and read the scrawled order. "Extra ranch."

Her gaze went to Rory at the end of the bar. He smiled at her, and she forgot what she was doing.

Jennifer rushed to the wait station and rechecked her notepad. She grabbed a premade side salad from the small refrigerator. Even out of his eyesight, it felt like Rory watched her. She ladled ranch onto the lettuce.

*"There you are."*

That voice!

Jennifer gasped and turned. No one was with her. She leaned to look out at the dining room.

"Not it. I took the last large party," Kay said, entering. "This one is yours."

Jennifer nodded, still shaky. "How many?"

"Ten." Kay grabbed a coffeepot to do refills and left.

Jennifer took a tray from a stack and made ten glasses of ice waters to bring to her new table. She had to get control of herself. She needed this job. Balancing the tray on her shoulder, she carried the waters and the salad out of the wait station.

Jennifer walked toward the redhead to drop off the salad. "Here you go."

"I didn't order this." The redhead frowned.

"What?" Jennifer still held the tray. "Extra ranch, right?"

"For my cheese fries," the woman snapped, her face becoming pinched in annoyance.

"Right, sorry, salad is on the house," she muttered. "Fries are coming."

"Who in all the blue blazes would want salad drenched in dressing?" the woman said to her husband as Jennifer walked away. "I don't think this one's going to earn a tip." Her voice rose as she loudly added, "I'll be surprised if she remembers my *mar-ga-rita*."

Jennifer frowned to herself.

*Crap. Don't forget the margarita.*

She turned to one of the few places they had set up for a table of ten and stopped mid-walk.

Rory stood next to Bruce and Maura and four other males who were undoubtedly related to him —the kilts were the most obvious giveaway, but their looks were a close second. There were also three women.

"Hi." Jennifer forced herself to approach the table and began setting waters before the customers.

"Hey, Jennifer," Maura said. "Good to see ya again."

Jennifer nodded.

*Don't forget the margarita.*

"Good to see you too." She held the now-empty tray braced against her waist and pulled her notepad out of her apron.

"Jennifer, meet some of my family," Maura introduced. "These are my cousins Erik, his wife Lydia, Iain, his wife Jane, Euann, his wife Cora, and Uncle Raibeart."

Jennifer tried to keep her smile, but there was

no way she was remembering all of those names. She couldn't remember the…

Damn it. What was she supposed to get?

"Pleasure to meet ya again, lassie." Raibeart stood from the head of the table and made a flourishing gesture with his hand. Jennifer stared at his hands, trying to remember where she might have seen them. "Ya might not remember me, but—"

"Glowing," she whispered.

"Aye. Glowing indeed," Raibeart answered. "So ya feel it too? Does that mean ya remember my offer?"

"What offer?" Jennifer had no idea what he was talking about.

"Raibeart, just…" Rory gestured at his uncle to sit down. "Pretend you're someone else."

"Like who?" Raibeart hunched his shoulders and mocked, his words slurring, "Look at me, I'm Rory. I have warts on my arse. I haven't had a date in three hundred years, and it's made me grouchy. Unless ya count my right ha—"

"Raibeart!" Maura scolded. "We can't take ya anywhere."

"Ya sounded just like your ma, right then," Raibeart said. "I'm going to call ya Little Cait."

"Don't make me tell my ma on ya, Raibeart," Maura warned.

"Do, and ya will be in as much trouble as I, Little Cait," Raibeart returned. "We're not supposed to be here tonight. Cait said we have to leave Rory alone. I guess she was worried the laddie wouldn't stand a chance with his Uncle Raibeart stealing the show. Ladies can't resist me."

"All right then," Maura said in apparent disbelief.

"It's true. Just today, I polled a forum full of sexy ladies and asked if they'd marry me. Every one of them said aye. I can prove it." He produced a cell phone from the sporran resting against the front of his kilt. "I made sure the poll blocked the group until they answered, too. That way, they wouldn't get too shy about it. Ya know how the ladies are around a handsome man."

"An internet poll?" Maura laughed. "What options did ya give them? Yes, aye, and hell yeah? Did ya even put a no option on there?"

"Why would I? Whose going to say no?" Raibeart scoffed. He continued to look at his phone screen. "I know that the group is here somewhere." He began mumbling to himself as he swiped. "Knitting forum, Michelle Pillow reader group—sounds familiar, but no, I don't think it's that—uh, used cars, tea party ideas, kilt enthusiasts, fire bagpipes, naked Scotland. Och, I almost forgot, I have new photos to post there."

Rory came around the table to face Jennifer as Raibeart distracted himself on his phone. "I had no idea they would all show up here tonight. I know Maura mentioned trying the nachos, but Raibeart heard I was here with ya, and he called the others to come spy on us."

Jennifer frowned. Admittedly, she felt attraction (and unreasonable anger) toward Rory, but that didn't mean they were worth spying on. It sounded a little like the guy from table twelve's family showing up because he thought the waitress he just met was pretty. It didn't make sense.

*Shit. Table twelve asked for…something.*

"It's fine. It's a restaurant. People come here to eat." She glanced around. The irritated redhead scowled at her.

*Martini. Don't forget the martini.*

"I apologize in advance for anything they might say or do," Rory insisted. "MacGregors are nothing if not chaotic."

Jennifer wanted to ask him to sit down far away from her so she could concentrate. The only chaos she felt was the effect he had on her emotions. Rory remained standing, and his nearness made it challenging to think. She found herself gripping her pen, resisting the urge to fling it at his head.

"Have you all decided or would you like time with the menus?" she asked them.

"Nachos," one of the women said. Jennifer didn't even try to remember her name.

*Was it a martini? Wait, no. Margarita.*

"Mm, yes, tater tot nachos," another MacGregor woman agreed.

"Three nachos," Maura said.

"Four," someone corrected.

"Cheeseburger, fries," one of the cousins ordered.

"Same," two people said in unison.

Jennifer felt her frustration toward Rory mounting. She tried to write it all down, but she pushed so hard that the pen tip tore into the paper.

"Sex on the Beach," Raibeart said. "And to drink, scotch on the rocks."

"Ya should bring him a Sex on the Beach and make him drink it as punishment for that tired joke," Maura said. "And bring me a martini, please."

*Another martini. No, margarita and martini.*

"Burger, extra pickles," Bruce added, shutting his menu. "Kettle chips, not fries."

"I want bacon cheese fries," Jane said. "Side of ranch."

*More ranch. Everyone wants ranch.*

"Club sandwich?" Euann mused, more to himself than to her, so it didn't sound like an order.

"Please," Jennifer whispered, shaking. There were too many voices all around her, too many orders. They kept talking, but she didn't hear them.

*Please slow down.*

*Please stop.*

*Please go away.*

*Please…*

*I can't. I can't. I can't.*

"Jennifer?" Rory asked, touching her elbow. "Are—"

*"There you are."*

She jerked at the contact and dropped the tray. The loud clatter caused instant silence to come over the restaurant.

"Job opening!" the bartender yelled, tapping a spoon loudly against a glass. A wave of laughter met his teasing, and the murmur of conversation resumed.

"Did you hear that?" Jennifer asked Rory.

"What? The bartender?" Rory glanced toward the bar. "Did he embarrass ya? Do ya want me to have a word with him?"

"What? No, Earl's harmless." She looked into Rory's concerned face. He didn't deserve her irritation. She lowered her voice so the others couldn't overhear. "Please, sit down. Relax. Have fun. There are only two of us on the floor tonight, and I have to keep moving. I'm behind, and I have to sort through these orders."

Considering her state of mind, she was rather proud she managed a polite excuse. When she tried to leave, he touched her arm to stop her.

"Rory, please," She pulled away from him. "I can't do this now. I don't know what's happening to me, and I can barely concentrate as it is. My emotions are all over the place. Something tells me you have answers, but I need to get through this shift first. I need this job."

"Of course," he said. "Don't worry about us. Take your time. We'll talk after your shift."

Jennifer nodded and moved away from him.

"Damn, Rory, she's paid to come to our table, and ya still can't get her to talk to ya," one of the MacGregor's teased him.

"Quiet, Uncle Chicken," Rory said. "She's busy. Show some manners."

Jennifer went to the computer to input her orders and found herself staring at it for a long moment.

"Some lady is asking if I can take over your table," Kay said beside her. "She said she ordered a margarita and cheese fries an hour ago. What's going on? Did you forget to put it in?"

Jennifer automatically turned to look in the direction of the redhead. "It's hardly been twenty minutes. I'm getting her damned margarita."

"Want me to spit in it?" Kay offered.

Jennifer forced a laugh. "Maybe later."

They would never do such a thing, but the idea was tempting. Jennifer studied her notepad and began keying in her backlog of orders. By the time she got to the MacGregors, she could only guess what they had wanted.

With her performance, tonight's tips were going to be some of the worst in history.

*Don't forget the margarita.*

# Chapter Ten

"How big is this place? I've heard about it, but I haven't seen it." Jennifer leaned to look out the passenger window as they turned off the city street onto the driveway.

Rory hoped that she would be able to relax a little. Any fool could see she'd had a hard work shift. Two tables had complained to Earl, who was acting manager for the night since the owner was gone. She'd messed up his family's order, though not as badly as some of her other customers'. He'd seen trays of food being sent back to the kitchen. The other waitress, Kay, had seemed annoyed with Jennifer. By the end of the night, Kay had stopped speaking to her.

"About eighty acres, something like that," he answered. "Not the house, obviously, that's only twenty thousand square feet, but the property includes all of this hill, a fair bit of forest, a stream, walking paths, cultivated gardens in the back, and an old coach house from the late eighteen hundreds that we converted into a garage."

Jennifer leaned farther out the window. The wind hit her face, wildly blowing locks of her hair that had come loose from the twist tie. Rory was more interested in watching her than the road. He pretended to drive while his magick guided the car up the curving driveway toward the mansion.

"Lydia owns the only other house on the hill," he said. "That's where she and Erik stay. She runs the business Love Potions out of it. Have ya heard of it?"

Jennifer shook her head in denial.

"All the women in the family seem to love it. They make homemade lotions, candles, teas, bath soaps, girly stuff. I'll take ya by there sometime if ya like."

"Yeah, maybe," she said, appearing as if she were trying to get a better look at the house as they drove closer.

Headlights shone in his rearview. Jennifer turned her head away from the side view mirror and sheltered her eyes. Euann came speeding past to beat them up the hill. Usually, Rory would race, but he let his cousin win this one. He knew once he'd reached the end of this drive, things would change drastically for Jennifer. He still hadn't figured out how to tell her magick was real. It's not a conversation they liked to have with mortals.

"We've been discussing putting in a golf course, but it would be a shame to cut down so many trees to make it happen."

There. Golf. Normal.

"Trees are better than golf," Jennifer said. "I can't stand it. Watching golf is like receiving a lobotomy in slow motion."

"Och, no lassie, don't let my family hear ya say that." Rory placed a hand over his heart. "Perhaps ya didn't have the right teacher."

"If that's an invitation, thank you, but I'll pass," she said. "So they say you all moved here recently."

"They?"

"They, people, townsfolk," she answered with a smile. That one expression lit up his whole body with pleasure.

"Aye, we did."

She sat back in her seat. Her hair still whipped a little from the wind but not as much as before. "Where did you move from? Scotland?"

"The family hasn't lived in Scotland for many, many years. We discuss going back at various times, but honestly, we've been here so long, America has become home."

"Where did you live before here?"

"New York, most recently. Before that in Philadelphia, and before that a Southern plantation, basically anywhere we can find big enough to fit us all. I think this area might be one of my favorites."

"Really? You have lived all over the world, and Wisconsin is your favorite?" She seemed skeptical. "From the pictures I've seen, Scotland would be amazing. I don't know how you left."

"We left when it was time to do so." Rory still didn't push a more serious conversation. "Finding a home that can fit us all with so much untouched beauty is rare. I have a feeling we'll be calling Green Vallis home for a long time."

He pulled up in front of the Georgian-style mansion, parking the car so that her door faced the house's front. Spotlights were aimed at the stark white siding, causing the home to practically glow against the dark sky.

"Holy crap, you are rich," Jennifer whispered.

"It's family money."

"Still…" She opened the door and slowly stepped out of his car. "I don't think I've ever met someone who could afford to live in a palace."

"It's hardly a palace."

"Um, I live in a seven-hundred-square-foot trailer." She tilted her head back to look toward the roof. "This is a twenty-thousand-square-foot house. A hundred of my homes could fit in here."

"Not quite that many," he denied. Rory started walking toward the house, expecting her to follow.

"Regardless, compared to where I live, this is a freaking palace." She took a deep breath and didn't look like she was going to go inside.

"What is it?" Rory walked back toward his car.

In the valley at the bottom of the hill, lights created a beautiful pattern. It was far enough to look like stars covering the earth but close enough that he could still make out which line of light was Main Street.

"Are ya embarrassed because ya live in a trailer? I guarantee that no one here will care," he said, trying to put her at ease.

"Why would I be embarrassed about that?" She frowned. "There's no shame in living in a trailer. Or being poor. I don't regret any of the decisions that have led me to where I am. Sure, if I would have gone to college, I might be making more money right now, but then I wouldn't have been there to take care of my dad for the last years of his life. I don't regret a second I got to spend with him. People win over material things any day of the week."

"I fully agree." Rory nodded. "But then, can I ask why ya look nervous?"

"I think there was someone in my home earlier," she said. "That's why I agreed to come here. I was too scared to go home, but I'm not sure…"

"Ya are most welcome to stay as long as ya need," he said. "My family can be a handful, as ya well saw, but they mean well."

"I'm not trying to move in," Jennifer assured him. She frowned and looked around the lawn. "Do you hear that?"

"What?" He didn't hear anything.

"You don't hear someone speaking?" She turned to a line of trees and inched toward them, craning her neck as if that might help her see past them.

"Only ya," he said. "Lydia's house is that way. Maybe she and Erik's voices are carrying?"

"No. I've been hearing this one all day." She frowned. "You don't hear another voice? A woman?"

"What's the woman saying?"

"There you are," Jennifer answered. "Over and over. There you are. It's like she's been looking for me but…I sound insane."

"You're not insane." Rory put his arm over her shoulders. "Let's go inside."

"I wouldn't be so sure. I swear, I saw your uncle's hands glow." Jennifer resisted going into the house with him. "I think maybe I hit my head the night you found me in the woods, and I should have gone to a doctor. That's the only explanation."

Rory furrowed his brow. "Well, not the *only*."

"The most likely, then," Jennifer insisted. "Audible hallucinations, lack of focus, trouble remembering people's orders, emotional distress."

"Emotional distress?" Rory found himself wanting to pull her closer. "What do ya mean by that?"

"When I'm near you, I…" She refused to meet his gaze.

"I feel the same way." Rory cupped her cheeks and pulled her in for a kiss. Pleasure and anticipation erupted inside of him.

"What?" Jennifer swatted at his hands. "I didn't mean I want to make out with you. I meant that when I'm near you, I want to hit you over the head with a bat."

"Ya don't want to…?" He pulled back.

Wow. He'd read that signal wrong.

"I mean, yeah, of course, I want to kiss you. You're handsome and nice and wear a kilt like some kind of romance movie hero. It's hard not to see the fantasy there." She took a step back. "But I also have this undeniably strong urge to run you over with a car."

"Sounds like marriage."

Rory stiffened to hear his father's voice coming from the front door.

"My Cait threatens to run me over all the time, though she usually says she wants to trample me with wild horses," Murdoch said. "Can't say I don't sometimes deserve it. Take my word for it, son. Apologize. It doesn't matter what for. Always assume when it comes to your woman's anger, you're in the wrong."

Rory flinched. Referring to Jennifer as his "woman" after she pulled away from his kiss probably wasn't the best flow of conversation.

"Da, I'd like ya to meet Jennifer," Rory introduced. "She's a friend."

"Mr. MacGregor." Jennifer gave a small wave but didn't go closer to the house.

"Murdoch," his father corrected. "Listen, son, your ma and aunt Margareta are waiting for ya in the dining room. They look serious. There's cheese and wine." He switched his language so Jennifer couldn't understand and added, "Plus, they are discussing binding spells, just in case."

"No, Da," Rory said, keeping to English so

Jennifer wouldn't be uncomfortable. "This was probably a mistake. I'm going to take her to the motel. Maura will love the company."

"Too late. Euann, Cora, and Raibeart already told them you're coming, and they saw your car pull up. Ya might as well come and get it over with." Murdoch smiled at Jennifer. "I promise it's not as painful as it sounds."

Jennifer smiled politely. "I'm sure everyone is very nice. I'm not worried."

"Then it's settled." Murdoch gestured for Jennifer to join them in the house. "Jennifer, do ya like wine?"

"Not as much as I like cheese," she answered.

"Perfect." Murdoch led the way into the house. "We have an assortment from all over the world."

"Ya don't have to," Rory said. "Everyone will understand if you're too tired after your double shift."

"I don't want to be rude to your family," Jennifer said.

"I don't want them to overwhelm ya," he answered. What had he been thinking to bring Jennifer here? Did he think his family would just let him waltz her up to a guest room?

Well, in truth, he hadn't been thinking about that. He'd been too busy trying to make sure she came with him someplace away from the public to talk to him. He couldn't exactly tell her what she needed to know while she was working. *"Oh, hey, by the way, I'm a warlock, magick is real, you're possessed, and table five needs beer when ya get a chance. Try not to freak out."*

"We haven't had a chance to talk about the forest," he said.

"Yes, we did. You said you found me on the ground. Did you lie? Was there more?" she asked.

Lie was such a harsh word, and yet…

"I'm not sure we completely understand what is happening," he said. "I think we should compare notes.

There. That wasn't a lie. It was an avoidance, but not a lie.

"Compare notes?" Jennifer chuckled. This time she walked up the front steps with Rory to go inside. "What is this? Math class?"

"I'm sorry for whatever is about to happen," Rory whispered.

"Why? What's about to happen? Wine and cheese and a chance to see inside the infamous MacGregor mansion?" Jennifer softly laughed. "This will give me something to talk about to entertain customers for the next couple of weeks, at the very least."

"I…" Rory wanted to tell her everything. "I know how overwhelming my family can be."

"You are worried about me being here, aren't you?" Jennifer touched his arm briefly before pulling her hand away and balling it into a fist. "Perhaps you're right to be. I don't exactly trust myself when I'm next to you. We can say hello to be polite, and then you can take me to the motel."

## Chapter Eleven

"This recipe is from right here in Wisconsin. It's an enchanting blend." Cait MacGregor held out a silver tray containing a cheese ball with a shaved almond crust surrounded by crackers. It looked like something served at a football party, not at an international cheese and wine tasting. If they brought out a box of wine next, Jennifer would know she was on a prank show.

"Looks great, Ma." Rory reached to take a cracker, but Cait slapped his hand. "Ladies first."

"Think of me as the royal taster," Rory answered.

"I raised ya with better manners than that," Cait warned.

Jennifer wasn't sure if Cait was serious or not,

but Rory looked properly scolded and withdrew his attempt.

Jennifer glanced at the tray they offered to her. Besides Rory's parents, his aunt Margareta and uncle Angus were also in the dining room. She heard activity in other parts of the house, but no one else came to join them. Aside from those footsteps and the subtle brushes of movement in the dining room when her hosts adjusted their stances, the place was quiet.

Too quiet.

Jennifer felt their eyes on her, studying her. She slowly reached for a cracker.

Cait and Margareta both nodded that she should try it.

Since Cait still held the tray, when Jennifer tried to scrape the firm cheese with the cracker, it snapped in half.

Murdoch cleared his throat. "I thought ya said we would be having cheeses from around the world."

"Wisconsin is part of the world last time I checked," Cait said.

"What about that nice Brie Fergus brought back from France? Or the Airedale from New Zealand?" Murdock suggested.

"Shh," Cait admonished, only to whisper loudly, "This is the first stop on the world tour."

"You're doing things out of order," Margareta added.

"My apologies," Murdoch muttered. "Though that doesn't explain the lack of wine."

"Then why don't ya fetch a bottle?" Cait urged, her pleasant smile tightening slightly.

Murdoch made a soft noise and walked out of the room.

The quiet house and the seriousness of the cheese conversation reminded Jennifer of all those quiescently boring sitcom scenes of people sitting in bed-and-breakfasts listening to a monotone voice talk about bird watching.

"I wanted to come in and meet all of you and thank you personally for the invitation, but I really should be going," Jennifer said.

"Knife," Cait stated.

"Excuse me?" Jennifer glanced at Rory for help.

"For the cheese, dear," Margareta said before Rory could speak.

Cait set the tray on the dining table and disappeared into another room. She came back with a butter knife. "Here we go."

Jennifer slowly took the knife the woman offered. They all watched her like she was to kick off the start of the festivities.

"Hey, I heard we're breaking open the New

Zealand Airedale." Raibeart appeared in the doorway with a grin. "I'll take a wedge of that."

"Ya aren't invited," Margareta said, shooing him from the room.

It didn't work. Raibeart dodged her hands when he saw Jennifer. "I see ya met my future bride. How's it going, love?"

"Wrong woman," Rory stated. "Your fiancée was out front. She didn't appear very happy with ya. I think she said she was taking to the woods."

Raibeart's eyes strangely caught the light as he glanced over his shoulder in the direction of the front door. "Excuse me." He rushed to go outside. The door slammed shut behind him.

"That was mean," Cait chastised Rory with a small laugh.

"My love?" The windowpane muffled Raibeart's yell.

Jennifer turned to peer out the window. "Oh!"

Raibeart streaked past as his kilt fluttered behind him to land on the lawn. He ran across the yard toward the forest.

"Not again." Margareta sighed. "I'll send Angus after him."

"We can do this later," Jennifer said. "If you need to—"

"He'll be fine. It's not the first time, and it

won't be the last." Cait gestured at the tray. "Try the cheese ball."

Jennifer took the knife, more out of duty than excitement, and cut a piece of the firm cheese before squishing it on top of a cracker. The speckled insides of the ball had a green tint to it. She lifted it to her mouth and bit.

"Mm," she nodded that it was good even before she tasted it. She set the knife down.

The cheese didn't have a distinct flavor. It wasn't awful, but it wasn't anything she'd crave.

"Here, try another," Margareta said, leaning over to put a giant glob on a cracker. "Really experience the full flavor."

Jennifer reached for the cracker, wanting to be polite to Rory's family. She stepped back to keep them from giving her a third one. She swallowed and started to lift the second hors d'oeuvre. Her mouth went numb like she'd been given a shot of Novocain.

Jennifer looked at the loaded cracker she held. Dark liquid dripped from her mouth onto the back of her wrist. She instantly touched her lips. Her fingers slipped in what felt like blood, and she pulled her hand back to look. Thick black coated her fingertips. Her hand shook violently.

She dropped the cracker onto the floor and reached to touch her mouth with her other hand, as if that would change the result. When she drew her fingers back, they were smeared with dark fibrous chunks.

Jennifer's eyes widened as she glanced at Rory. His lips moved, but she couldn't hear what he said. Margareta frowned at her. Cait pointed at her face.

She turned in fear, only to catch her reflection in the windowpane. Black dripped out her eyes like tears. Her mouth filled with numbed pressure, and it became hard to breathe.

"Ma tell me ya didn't try to make that thing yourself. Not for company!" Rory's panicked voice sounded far away and came beneath the buzzing in her ears. "What did ya put in the recipe?"

Jennifer bent forward and coughed. Rory patted her back. A muddy clump dropped past her lips into her hands. She gasped for breath. It slid off her shaking hand onto the floor.

*What the hell?*

How were they not reacting to this? Didn't they see she was throwing up mud?

"Ror…" His name barely made it past her lips as she swayed and stumbled her way out of the dining room door.

"Where are ya going, dear?" Cait asked.

Jennifer tripped over the threshold and landed on her hands and knees on the hard marble of the foyer. Pain radiated up from her knees and wrists. She coughed again, spewing the dark clumps over the clean floor.

*"There you are."*

The voice had returned.

Desperate, she crawled toward the door to escape. The pressure spread from her mouth to her throat and she tried to gasp for a breath that wouldn't come.

"Jennifer?"

*Snap. Snap.*

"Jennifer?"

*Snap.*

Jennifer gasped a high-pitched sound as she reached for her throat.

Cait leaned close to her face.

Margareta dropped her hand from where she'd been snapping her fingers beside Jennifer's ear.

"There ya are, dear." Cait smiled. "Welcome back. Ya gave us quite a scare."

*There you are.*

The terrifying voice whispered through her mind.

Jennifer pushed up in her cushioned chair. The furniture's feet slid from the force of her movement, making a loud noise against the rug.

Rory came from behind her as if to steady her.

He held her by the back of her elbow. "Try to take it easy."

Jennifer looked around in confusion. Books lined a wall of dark shelves. Curtains covered a large window. Light came from a couple of table lamps. The green glass panels of the shade casting patterns on the ceiling.

Margareta and Cait stood watching her, heads tilted to the side ever so slightly, with matching pod-people expressions. She expected alien heads or robot parts to spring past their plastered smiles at any moment.

"How did I get in here?" Jennifer asked. Then, remembering her numb mouth, she frowned. "What did you dose me with?"

"Dose?" Margareta gave a weak laugh.

"Ya fainted, dear," Cait said.

Jennifer pulled her hand from Rory. "I'm not an idiot. What was in that cheese?"

"Herbs," Cait said.

"Spices," Margareta added.

"Ma, Aunt Margareta, stop," Rory ordered.

"Rory don't cause a scene," Cait said to her son, her teeth gritting just enough to cause her fake smile to falter.

"Are ya allergic to—?" Margareta began, trying to act all innocent.

"Bullshit?" Jennifer quipped.

Margareta gasped a little at her bluntness.

"Yeah, Margareta, I am allergic to bullshit. Thanks for asking." Jennifer jerked her arm from Rory. "I'm leaving. Can't say it was a pleasure to meet either of you."

Jennifer felt her rage mounting. It was all she could do to keep the anger at bay next to Rory but faced by whatever roofie Cait and Margareta had slipped into her food; it came pouring out of her. Her limbs trembled, and she knew if she didn't get out of there fast, she'd do something she regretted.

"Wait," Cait tried to protest.

"Jennifer," Margareta said as if to call her back.

Jennifer heard footsteps following her and walked faster. She didn't know where she was going, but she found herself in the front hall next to the giant staircase when she left the library.

"Jennifer," Rory called, following her.

She walked faster toward the front door.

"Jennifer," he insisted.

"What's happening?" a voice called from above.

"Not now, Euann," Rory said.

"Ah, did ya mess it up with her already?" Euann teased with a laugh. "I think that's a world record, even for ya, cousin."

"Shut up, Euann!" Rory insisted. "Not now, Ma. Ya have done enough damage."

Jennifer tried to jerk the front door open, and her hand slipped off the knob. She wasn't in the mood for teasing or talking or this freaking door. She grabbed the knob with both hands, but it wouldn't budge. In anger, she shook it violently. "Let me out of here!"

"Rory, what happened?" Euann's voice became concerned.

Rory appeared beside her. She jerked away from him. He lifted his hands, fingers spread to show he meant no harm as he slowly reached past her to turn the deadbolt lock on the door. He then pulled the knob to open it for her.

Jennifer rushed out of the house. Her heart beat faster. She didn't think past the need to get away from the mansion. She ran past Rory's car and headed down the driveway.

"Jennifer, wait, I can give ya a ride wherever ya want to go. Don't leave like this." Rory called after her. "Please, just take a breath and try to calm down. I can explain."

"Calm down?" She stumbled and caught herself before turning to face him as he came after her. "Calm down! You know, Rory, all women know not to leave a drink unattended at a bar. It's one of the sad realities of being female. We open our own drinks, even water bottles, or watch it being made for fear someone will slip us a Mickey. I know how to live on my own as a woman and protect myself, but apparently, I missed the lesson on not taking cheese from strangers."

"Slipped a mickey?" He started to shake his head in denial.

"Slip a mickey, roofie, Mickey Finn, micked, knock-out drops, GHB, Rohypnol, Ketamine, LSD, what-ever-the-fuck——" she yelled.

"I can explain," he tried to insert.

"——they put into that food," she continued, pointing angrily toward the mansion. "You know they did. They didn't want you eating it but were super high-pressure that I should try it. There is no satisfying explanation for that. I'm going to the police. I'm going to make them give me a blood test. You can't treat people like this. I don't care if you are rich and live in a castle."

"They were trying to help ya purge," he said.

*Purge? What the hell?*

"Purge what? My insides? My sanity?" She shook her head. "I don't know what kind of crap you're used to getting away with, but——"

"Purge evil intent." He tried to reach for her.

"Evil? Are you fucking kidding me?" she cried. The release of outrage felt great, like a dam had broken free on her feelings, and all the pent-up emotions came out on her like a churning lava-fueled river.

"I know ya don't want to hear it right now, and I don't blame ya for being mad, but their hearts were in the right place. It…it backfired a little. Please, I can explain this better. Give me a chance to—"

"You're right. I don't want to hear it," Jennifer denied. She resumed her escape down the long driveway. The lights from town called her like a beacon, giving her context to where she needed to go. "If I require some kind of spiritual evil-purging journey, I'll find a qualified shaman, not a freaking football party rubbery cheese ball—that wasn't even all that amazing, to be honest."

Actually, a shaman might not be a bad idea. Or psychic ghost-hunter. Someone to stop the creepy voice from following her around. A shrink?

"Jennifer, stop, there's so much that ya don't understand yet," Rory said. "Things I didn't want to have to tell ya if I was wrong. Things I couldn't tell ya because…because some secrets have to be kept to protect my family."

Jennifer skidded to a stop and took a deep breath. Light flashed behind her and cast her shadow on the ground, haloed in soft blue glow. She assumed he had his phone flashlight app shining for them.

"What secrets?" She turned to face him again.

Rory stood with his hand held out. The soft blue glow came from his palm. She'd assumed it was his phone, but as the light radiated from a sphere, she stared into it.

"Glowing fingers," she whispered, pointing as if he'd need clarification for what she saw. Her hand shook. "I saw glowing…"

She took a backward step down the incline of the drive, then another.

"There you are," she whispered.

"It's a big secret I need to tell ya," Rory said. "But the simplest way is for me to show ya that magick is real. I'm a warlock. All MacGregors are warlocks."

What he was saying was ridiculous, of course. Warlocks? Magick? And yet, his hand glowed.

He bounced the ball of light between his hands before making a fist and extinguishing it. He lifted his hands, showing her the backs and fronts. They were empty.

The rage inside her centered itself in her chest, burning. Her breathing deepened.

The light returned to both hands, snaking from his fingers to his wrists, circling them like bracelets.

"There you are." The words passed her lips louder than before.

The ball of rage spread like flames down her arm, tingling her fingers. She lifted her hand to find she gripped a knife.

"Whoa." Rory started to lift his hands, but the magick glow became brighter on his wrists. The two light streams snaked toward the ground, pulling him to his knees like two shackles staked to the earth.

A feeling whispered inside of her, urging her to act without reason.

"There you are," she said. The words felt like a spell, winding through her. If she would only do what it wanted, it would leave her alone. She'd be safe.

Safe from harm.

Safe from Rory.

Safe from magick.

Safe.

The anger made it easy to strike. She felt the blade. All it needed was a small swing, and the sharp edge would do the rest.

"Jennifer, ya don't have to do this," Rory pleaded. He struggled against the magick holding him down.

Jennifer saw her arm moving, felt the knife jerk as the blade caught in his neck. Blood came from the wound, spraying over her. Rory's mouth opened, and his eyes met hers as if surprised she'd done it.

*No!*

This wasn't what she wanted. She wasn't a killer.

Jennifer blinked only to find he was still in front of her. The blood was gone, and the murderous urge had not yet played itself out. Rory was safe.

She blinked again, and he was on the ground, the magick on his wrists fading as blood pooled. Time made no sense. The pieces were scattered like a jigsaw puzzle someone threw on the floor.

*Blink.* He pleaded with her to stop.

*Blink.* Screams came from the house. His mother cried out in agony for her dying son. She and Margareta charged across the yard.

*Blink.* Rory was telling her he was a warlock. The magick had yet to bind him to the ground.

*Blink.* She swung her arm to kill him.

*Blink.* Trees passed her as she ran in the forest with bloodstained hands. Magick balls flew past her head as Cait and Margareta tried to capture her.

*Blink.* She was back in front of Rory.

*Blink.* He was dead.

*Blink.* He lived.

*Blink. Blink. Blink. Blink…*

The rage inside her erupted, urging her to get it over with, promising in some innate way that if she killed him, it all would stop.

She waited for the right piece of time to appear and finally found him kneeling with his magickal restraints. Jennifer forced her eyes to remain open, not letting go of the moment.

"Jennifer, please, listen to me. Ya can control the urges," Rory insisted.

"There you are." It was the only words that would come out of her mouth. Her hand trembled, ready to strike.

"Jennifer…"

"There you are." She stepped toward him. Every muscle acted as if she had no control.

"Please, I promise, I would never hurt ya," he said.

"There…" Jennifer tried to bite back the word. She held the knife over her shoulder, arm trembling with the effort it took not to stab forward. She fell to her knees before him. Her eyes burned with the need to blink.

"I don't know if ya can hear me, but this is what we were trying to stop. Please, let us help ya." Rory's eyes searched hers.

Jennifer tried to make herself drop the knife, but her fingers wouldn't release the hilt. When she was near him, he roused strong emotions. This rage she felt inside of her like an invading entity wasn't hers. She didn't hate like this. She felt guilty after squishing spiders. Now she wanted to murder Rory?

She watched his lips move, saying her name. He'd been nothing but kind to her—well, except for the cheese thing. Expelling mud had been disgusting.

"There you are," she whispered.

Jennifer didn't want to hurt him.

This wasn't her.

"There—"

She pressed her mouth to his and cut off her own words. His lips parted in a plea, and it provided for an instantly deeper kiss. The pleasure of fulfilling one of the stronger desires inside of her finally allowed her to release the blade. It dropped from her like a weight, and she reached to hold his face in her palms.

She struggled to keep from blinking, not wanting to erase what was happening.

Rory moaned, leaning into the kiss. His tongue darted past her lips. The pent-up energy needed a place to go, and it made its way into their embrace. She gripped his face tight as if the movements of her mouth could serve as a punishment. Rage and passion. She'd never understood just how linked those two emotions could be until this moment.

Jennifer's pulse raced. She heard her heart pounding a rhythm in her ears. It deafened her to all else. Everything about him overwhelmed her and captured her attention. She felt the heat of his body, the rough texture of the beard trying to shadow his jaw, the moistness of his mouth, and the tickle of his hair on the backs of her fingers.

When finally her lungs felt as if they would explode, she pulled away to gasp for breath. Sometime during the kiss, she'd forgotten to keep her eyes open, and now that they were closed, she was afraid to look.

"…you are," she whispered, finishing the words that had been forced from her lips.

He touched her arms, and she gasped, opening her eyes. They kneeled on the driveway. Cobblestones pressed uncomfortably into her knees.

"Jennifer?" Rory's gaze moved over her face.

"I can't tell what's real," she whispered, unwilling to let go of him. "Tell me, is this happening? Is this real?"

His hands covered hers on his face. "I'm real. This is real."

A tear slipped down her cheek. Maybe she wasn't as sane as she thought. A woman could only take so much—intruders, voices, lost time, liquid rage.

"I don't want to kill you," she said.

Rory gave a soft laugh. "That's good to hear, love. I wasn't too sure there for a moment."

How could he be smiling and laughing at a time like this? Her emotions were a tattered mess.

"I don't know where the anger comes from," she said. "It's not mine. I don't hate like this."

"If it makes ya kiss me like that, I think I like it when ya are mad at me," Rory answered.

"I'm serious, Rory," she scolded.

"So am I." He glanced down. "Feel beneath my kilt if ya don't believe me."

Jennifer caught herself automatically glancing down. It was difficult to see any shapes beneath the thick material, but his meaning wasn't lost on her. He kept her hands against his face, keeping her close to him.

Despite the very prurient interest her body had in taking him up on the offer, her mind concentrated on maintaining a semblance of control. "Do you take anything seriously?"

"Believe me, when it comes to pleasing a woman, I take my duties very seriously." His voice dipped, and when he looked her over, she felt as if he undressed her with his eyes. It stirred the already rampant desire bubbling inside of her. "And I'm very good at it."

Damn him.

Just damn him.

"Rory, I'm not joking. Something is wrong with me." Jennifer tried to pull her hands away from his face. He held her to him a few moments longer but finally released her.

"The only thing wrong is that for someone or something is using bad magick on ya, forcing ya to do things. It's not your fault," Rory said. "And I promise we're going to stop it. I won't let anyone or anything hurt ya."

Jennifer slowly stood. She eyed the knife on the ground and stepped several paces away from it. "Raibeart was in the woods. He had magick on his hands like you did. He hit me with it to stop me."

"Yes." Rory nodded. "To save me."

"That's why you didn't bring me to a doctor."

"There was nothing the hospital or the police could do for ya." Rory was slower to stand. He also looked at the weapon lying on the ground and put himself between her and the blade. "I wanted to tell ya, but…"

He lifted his hand. She expected to see the blue light erupt.

"Magick is real." Jennifer took a deep breath

and held it. "Out of all the explanations for what I've been feeling, I don't know if that one makes me feel better or worse. If not magick, then I have some real psychological issues. But if it's real, then, well, I'm not sure what then."

"Run!"

Jennifer jumped in surprise as a Raibeart burst through the trees behind her and took off up the drive. He had his hands cupped over his manhood.

"Raibeart!" Murdoch leaped from the trees and chased after him. His shirt was ripped, but he still wore his kilt and boots.

"They're after me dangly jewels!" Raibeart cried. Instead of going to the front door, he ran toward the side of the house. He disappeared around the corner.

Murdoch darted past his son. "Run!"

*"Gremahdamma."*

*"Damma-damma."*

Rory's eyes widened at the monstrous chatter. He shot toward her and grabbed her hand. "Run!"

"What?" Jennifer tried to look into the trees, but Rory hauled her toward the house.

She heard the patter of tiny feet behind them. Rory led the way to the side of his car.

"Down," he ordered as he tugged her to the

ground. He wrapped his arms around her, shielding her with his body as he held her against the tire.

"*Damma-damma*," a creature cackled.

Jennifer watched Murdoch from under Rory's arm as he disappeared from view chasing after Raibeart.

Heavy thumps landed on Rory's car seconds before a hoard of knobby little creatures jumped over their heads and continued after Raibeart and Murdoch. She'd never seen anything like it, at least not outside of a horror movie.

As the thumps on Rory's car ended, he slowly pulled up to check.

"*Damma*!" A straggler came over the car, brushing over Rory's hair.

"Oh, ow," Rory grunted as the creature used his hair to control the trajectory of its landing.

"What is that?" Jennifer whispered as the tiny creature faced them.

"Gremian," Rory said.

"Gremlin?" Jennifer kept her back pressed against the wheel.

"Gremian," Rory corrected. He put himself in front of her to create a shield between her and the small attacker. His fingers began to glow, and he cocked his arm back. "Close."

The gremian chattered as it ambled toward

them. It sniffed in her direction. Its tiny eyes widened, and it screeched as it hurried after its friends.

"What the…?" Jennifer stared where it disappeared.

"Huh, he seemed scared of ya," Rory observed.

"Of me?" Jennifer shook her head in disbelief.

"They're gone, come on." Rory pulled her to her feet. "Let's get inside."

Jennifer looked to make sure there weren't any more coming for them. The driveway was clear. She glanced at Rory's car. Dents dotted the hood.

She stumbled a little to keep up with him. "They wrecked your car."

"Don't worry about it. It's just a car." He steadied her elbow and escorted up the stairs.

Jennifer's heart beat frantically, and her chest was beginning to hurt. The stress of going from rage to lust to terror was taking its toll on her. She pushed her hand to her chest and didn't fight Rory as he pulled her back inside the mansion.

Euann and Margareta appeared to be waiting for them near the main entrance. The second the door opened, their conversation stopped.

"You're back," Margareta said. "Good."

"What happened to ya two?" Euann asked, his gaze moving to the top of her head.

Jennifer self-consciously reached for her hair and began smoothing it.

"I think it's about time we cleared the gremian problem out of the woods," Rory said. She noticed his hair was a little messy from the gremian, but he didn't seem to notice.

"Why? They're harmless, mostly. The humans can't see them," Euann said, pulling out his phone as if not concerned. "Plus, they usually only torment Uncle Raibeart."

"They're multiplying," Rory said.

"Are ya sure Raibeart's not the father?" Euann held his phone toward them and laughed as he walked closer so they could see it. A video played showing a gremian with a miniature wedding dress snuggled next to a passed out Raibeart. "I think one of them has a crush."

"What?" Margareta snatched the phone. "Who gave that hideous thing a—is that Cait's antique doll dress?"

"I'm human," Jennifer interrupted. "You said humans couldn't see them, but I saw them."

"Well, ah…" Margareta frowned and looked at Rory.

"I am human," Jennifer insisted.

"Ya look pretty human to me," Euann said. "Now, Rory, not so much. Ya know, Jenn, I have other cousins if ya are in the market for—"

"Aunt Margareta, Euann gave the gremian the doll dress," Rory interrupted, clearly to get his cousin into trouble.

"I did not," Euann protested. "Ma, he's lying."

"Why don't ya show your friend someplace to lay down," Margareta told Rory. "She looks like she's about to fall over. We can sort everything out in the morning."

Jennifer liked the idea of getting away from Margareta the cheese ball pusher, so didn't protest when Rory motioned for her to go upstairs with him. She also didn't want to go back outside in the dark with those creepy little monsters running around. As they reached the second story, she whispered, "Seriously, though, I am human. They know that, right?"

Rory led her down a hall and opened a door. "Ya can stay in my room."

At that, she looked inside to see a king-sized bed. Jennifer arched a brow. "I'd be suspicious that this was your intention all along, but I don't think there was any way you could fake those gremlins."

"Gremians," he said. The smile that curled his lips invited her back for more kisses. "I'll sleep elsewhere if—"

Jennifer pulled him by his shirt to bring him

into the room with her. "There is no way in hell you are leaving me alone in this place. If those gremians come back, I'm feeding you to them and running for my life."

"And here I was worried ya didn't like me," Rory teased.

## Chapter Twelve

Jennifer more than "liked" Rory. Liked seemed too tame of a word. When it came to Rory, her emotions ran hot—rage and lust. Neither state of being lent itself to rational decision making. Until she dropped that knife on the driveway, anger had been winning. Now with it dissipated, passion took over.

The world no longer made sense. Before Rory, she'd settled into a mundane routine of survival. She worked to pay bills. She paid bills to live. She lived to work so she could afford to pay bills. Round and round it went—paycheck to paycheck. Jennifer focused on what needed to be done right in front of her. In that way, her world had become very, very small.

Rory's world was enormous. Family money

clearly took away the live-work-bill cycle, but it was more than that. He had different responsibilities. He had family and magick and gremians to worry over. After seeing those hideous creatures, she wondered what else was out in the woods that she didn't know about. The possibilities seemed endless.

"Why are ya looking at me like that?" Rory stood in front of the bedroom door. The polished wood contrasted the white of the walls. That single bedroom was bigger than her entire trailer. A private bathroom could be seen in through the shadows of an opened door. The overhead lights' low-watt bulbs added to the intimacy, which would only be romantically outdone if he lit the fireplace.

The mattress was high off the ground, and she had to give a little hop to sit on the foot of his bed. "You don't find it weird that your parents live in the same house as you?"

He shook his head. "Why would I? Many extended families live together."

"I meant when you bring women home." Jennifer gave a nervous laugh.

"I don't generally bring women home," he said.

"I wasn't fishing about your dating life." Even

so, Jennifer liked hearing he wasn't in the habit of entertaining women in his bedroom.

"Fish all ya like, love." He grinned, closing the distance between them. His voice dipped with meaning. "I'm sure you'll catch something."

Jennifer's tone matched his. "I don't think that's as seductive as you think it is."

His smile didn't falter. The man did not lack in confidence. He traced the tip of his finger along her jaw.

Jennifer felt a shiver work its way over her. "Aren't you afraid I'll try to hurt you again?"

Rory leaned in and shook his head in denial. His eyes stared intently into hers. "I'm more afraid of what will happen if I don't kiss ya again."

"That sounds like a line," she whispered.

"It is," he agreed. "Is it working?"

Jennifer nodded. It was working. She wanted to kiss him again.

No, she *needed* to kiss him again.

At first, the depth of her desire frightened her, and she worried that it might be like the anger— something put inside her by magickal forces.

And yet, this felt different. When he touched her, she felt every nerve stand at attention. Her skin tingled with anticipation. All other concerns fell away until there were only the seconds flickering past as his mouth pressed against hers. Her eyes drifted close. His hands cupped her face.

Unlike on the driveway, this kiss was gentle, probing, testing. Rory brushed his lips along hers several times before parting them. With each stroke, the kiss became more profound. The tip of his tongue swept her bottom lip, enticing hers to join him.

"I should take a shower," she whispered against him.

His hand left her cheek seconds before she heard the water running in the bathroom.

Jennifer broke the kiss and turned her attention toward the noise. "How…?"

He lifted his hand and wiggled his fingers. Blue lights wove over them before disappearing. "Magick."

"What else can those fingers do?" Only after she said the words did she realize just how provocative they sounded.

"Do ya want me to show ya?"

How could she say no to the promise in his eyes? The idea of magick both thrilled and terrified her. It was those warring emotions that caused her heart to beat faster. There was danger here, but she didn't care. She wanted to jump into the deep end.

Jennifer nodded. "Show me."

Rory brought his glowing finger toward her neck. She felt the warmth and energy flowing from him into her, connecting them as it penetrated her. Slowly, he drew his hand down the front of her work shirt. The material appeared to melt from her body.

Her initial reaction was to gasp and cover her chest as if that could stop the reaction. She heard the sound of her shirt dropping on the floor beneath her feet.

"Shall I continue?" He looked down to where her arms crossed her breasts.

Slowly, she nodded, eager to see more of his magick. She lowered her arms.

He ran his fingers along her waist. The pleasurable warmth of his touch spread over her hips, settling erotically in her belly. The pants slithered onto the floor to join the shirt. Realizing she still wore shoes and socks, she kicked them off her feet and then knocked them with her heels under the bed.

Rory had left her in her bra and panties. The bedroom air felt cool compared to his magickal touch and the heat from his deepening breaths tickling her shoulder.

"Impressed?" He caressed her naked hip, hooking a finger in her panties.

Jennifer chuckled. "Hardly."

It was a lie. Of course, she was impressed. The guy melted her clothing off.

"I can do the same trick," Jennifer said. "Close your eyes."

Rory instantly obeyed. Jennifer studied his handsome face as she reached for his shirt and pulled it up over his head. He laughed as she tossed it on the floor.

"Ta-da!" She lifted her arms over her head as if she'd just performed a carnival magic trick.

Rory tilted his head back and laughed. The sound rained over her in pure delight. "Impressive."

As her hands lowered, she let them rest on his naked shoulders. Strong muscles moved beneath his warm flesh. Even without his magick, he was something to behold.

The sound of the shower caught her attention, and she pushed his shoulders so that he stepped back. She slid off the end of the bed. "I worked a double. I need that shower."

Jennifer walked toward the shower, reaching behind her back to unhook her bra as she moved. She dropped it on the floor.

Steam filled the bathroom. The shower curtain hung over a clawfoot tub. She reached behind it to test the water against her hand.

Rory touched her hip, startling her. She hadn't heard him step up behind her.

"Are you joining me?" she asked, not turning to face him.

"If ya are inviting me to," he answered.

Jennifer pushed her panties from her hips and stepped into the tub. There was something special about the first blast of hot water after a long day. She closed her eyes and took a deep breath.

"We just met," she said, hearing him come in behind her.

"Doesn't feel like it to me." Rory ran a finger down her spine, causing her to shiver. "But if ya want, I can sleep in the other room and come back tomorrow to take ya out on a proper date."

Jennifer did not want that. She turned to face him. He was completely naked, and she couldn't help glancing down at the thick arousal standing tall between them. It didn't appear like he wanted that either, but it was sweet that he respected her enough to offer.

"What? You don't think losing my mind and trying to stab you is a proper first date?" Though she teased, she managed to keep a serious expression. "So far, I would say it's in my top five first dates."

The hot water hit her back. It cascaded over

her shoulders and down her chest. He watched his hand slide against her breast to disrupt the flow. They might not have known each other long in the measurement of time, but somehow that didn't matter. She felt him on a deep, intimate level. She looked at him, and she just *knew* he was who she was meant to be with. The certainty of such a thought should have scared her, but it didn't.

"Top five?" His eyes darted up to hers as if finally processing what she said.

"Top three," she amended. "Number two was in the third grade. Joey Antonelli and I were forced to be study buddies. He serenaded me with country songs, and then after I checked 'no' on the little note he gave me asking me out, he told everyone I had warts and tried to kiss him."

"Smooth play, Mr. Antonelli. The night is young. I bet I can still beat him for that number two slot." Rory smirked, nodding. "And number one?"

"Blind date right after high school, Jimmy Jones. I remember because of like Jim Jones, the cult leader. Asshole ordered the most expensive thing, halved the bill to make me help pay for his meal, and then hit me with his car when we were leaving the restaurant."

"Was there a lot of damage to your vehicle?" Rory asked.

"He hit *me* with his car, not my car. He backed into me and knocked me on my backside. Left me with a bruised tailbone and a torn dress."

Rory leaned closer and let his hand glide from her breast down her side, only to snake around to cup her ass. "Feels like it healed all right, but I'll happily hex this Jimmy Jones for ya."

"You can do that? Hex people?" Jennifer was more curious than worried.

Rory nodded. "For ya? Anything. Just say the word."

"That's a sweet offer, but karma already got him. The woman he married ran over his foot."

He drew her body against his. Their naked flesh slid against each other in the water. Each tiny movement brought with it a myriad of sensations. Jennifer lost all thoughts as pleasure and temptation flooded her. She wanted this, him, more than anything else in her life.

"This is a bizarre conversation to be having at such a moment." Rory's lips brushed against her temple.

"What should we be talking about?" She found it hard to concentrate when she'd rather be kissing him.

"Soap."

"Soap?" she repeated, leaning back to study his face.

MICHELLE M. PILLOW®

"Mm." His lids fell heavy over his eyes as he reached his hand between the curtains only to return holding a bottle. "Definitely soap."

Rory squeezed a large amount on his hand and instantly brought his palms together to create the start of a lather. Magick glowed from his fingers as he brought the soap to her chest and began washing her. The soap glided while the magick tingled. The unmistakably male scent of the body wash smelled like him. When his hands slid around her hips to pull her against him, he washed her chest with his. The erotic play made it impossible to think beyond the moment.

Jennifer soaped her hands on his chest and drew them over his shoulders to his neck. She offered her mouth for a kiss. At times, she couldn't tell if he was washing her or caressing her, but either way it was gratifying. By the time his hands found their way between her thighs she was ready to scream from sexual need.

The tingling touch of his magick-laced fingers was unlike anything she'd ever felt. When he touched her, there were no doubts or fears. When he kissed her, she felt safe and protected. This is what perfection felt like.

No, not perfection. Love. This is what love felt like.

The concept seemed strange, to love someone

without the history, the type of connection that usually took time to build. And yet, Jennifer felt love for him, and part of her thought maybe he could love her too.

A finger stroked along her sex, tingling and rubbing, sliding in her body's natural response. It didn't take much for an orgasm to flow through her. She gasped, forced to grab hold of his arms to keep from falling in the tub.

"Oh my…" She tried to form the words, but they wouldn't come. "Wow."

"Oh my wow to ya too, love," Rory whispered. She felt the heat of his arousal against her stomach. He had not joined her in release. "That was a beautiful thing to behold."

"We should, ah, should…?" Jennifer gave a small laugh. "What?"

"Turn around, rinse off," he said.

She nodded, turning to wash the remainder of the soap from her skin. She pushed her wet hair over her shoulders only to feel him start to lather it for her. When he finished, he said, "Turn." She did, rinsing her hair. They repeated the processing with the conditioner.

Like a gentleman, he helped her step out of the tub before rinsing himself and following her. Jennifer dried with a towel. Rory didn't bother to get his own as he grabbed one end of her towel and pulled her toward the bed.

Rory urged her onto the mattress, throwing the towel aside as he crawled over with damp skin. The eagerness of his movements gave away the desperation of his desires. He had not met with his release in the shower.

The soft comforter padded the length of her body as a naked thigh pressed between her legs. He brought his mouth to hers, resuming where they'd left off in the shower. The sounds of his moans caused her to shiver. Each brush of his body to hers left trails of magick in its wake.

Jennifer opened her legs, needing to feel him.

"Don't worry, I have protection," he whispered seconds before a glow came from between them. She glanced between their bodies to see from where the light came.

Jennifer couldn't help her laugh. "A glowing penis. I can definitely say that's a first."

Rory tried to smile, but the look appeared pained as he maneuvered his hips between her thighs and pushed forward. She waited in anticipation, wondering if that part of him would tingle like the rest when it touched her. Jennifer gasped as a pulse of energy vibrated as he entered her. It coursed through her like electric fire, sizzling her from her head to her toes in overwhelming passion.

Even without the magickal bonus, Rory knew how to please her, working his hips, lifting and thrusting, kissing and moaning. She felt as if she were the center of his world.

Jennifer made a soft noise as the tension built toward another release. Her heart hammered violently. She trembled as the climax ripped through her. Rory stiffened above her as he too found release.

Jennifer tried to catch her breath. Her arms dropped over her head on the comforter. "Oh my. Wow."

Rory rolled to lie next to her on the bed. He pulled her by the hip to move her closer to him. He gazed into her eyes for a long time. When their breathing finally slowed, he whispered, "I don't know how to say this without sounding cheesy or scaring ya away, but…"

"But?" She prompted, eagerly awaiting for him to finish the thought.

"I have been around a long time. Hundreds of years," he said.

"Ah…?" Jennifer considered that. It's not what she had expected him to say, but it was knowledge she should probably have. "So, you're like immortal?"

"Long life span," he corrected. "Warlocks can be killed."

"You mentioned that before. What exactly does that mean, you're all warlocks?" Jennifer was too relaxed to be frightened by long life spans, and it was a little late to freak out about magick at this point.

"My siblings and cousins and I were born magicks," he said. "Others marry into the family, and over time, the natural-born warlocks' life spans and powers transfer to our spouses in different ways. My ma, for example, is very adept at potions and tapping into the magick for herself. She's been doing it so long she doesn't need my father around to fuel her."

"Wait, are you saying since we…?" Excited, Jennifer sat up from the bed and lifted her hand. She concentrated on her fingers, trying to make them glow.

"What are ya doing?" he asked.

When it didn't work, she frowned. "Well, that kind of sucks. I thought you were telling me that since we had sex, I would be able to do something cool and warlocky."

"Hey!" He tugged her arm to force her back down next to him. He rested on his back as she leaned next to him on her side. "Sex with me *is* the something cool."

She laughed and teased, "I mean, it's all right, but it's no making finger fire."

He chuckled. "Hold out your hand."

Jennifer remained on her side and instantly lifted her hand into the air above him. He formed a light ball in his palm and bounced it a few times before sliding it to her hand. She gasped as she felt it against her palm, churning like a living thing. She held it close to her face to look into the depths.

"It's beautiful," she whispered.

"You're beautiful," he said.

The light slowly began to fade, dying in her palm. "Where does it go?"

"Back into the universe," he said. "Magick is just energy. It must come from somewhere, and it must go somewhere."

"Where does it come from?" She wondered if she could learn to tap into it.

"That's a complicated question, but the short answer is to create magick I have to borrow the energy from something—like plant life. That's why my family moved here. Nature allows us to use just a little from each plant as fuel so that we don't kill anything.

"So what I felt was plant life?"

"What ya felt was sexual energy." He grinned.

Jennifer laughed. "I'm being serious. Was that a plant I was holding?"

"I'm serious too. Sexual energy can fuel magick, but like a climax, it burns hot and doesn't last as long as nature."

"I was holding sex?" She wagged her brows at him.

He took her hand and brought her fingers to his lips. He kissed the tips before leading her hand down his stomach toward his cock. "Now ya are holding my sex."

Jennifer laughed even as she felt him stirring with interest. She pulled her hand away and adjusted on the covers into a more comfortable position. Normally women joked that men needed a moment to recover between bouts, but after two intense orgasms, Jennifer was the one who needed a breather.

"I was trying to explain something," he said, lazily touching her chest and tracing a nipple. "When I said I had a long life, I meant I have been around long enough to know what I feel."

Her breath caught slightly as she waited for him to continue.

"I know humans aren't always as…" He seemed to struggle to find the right words.

"You're not going to insult me. Just say it," she urged.

"Humans aren't always as forthcoming—or maybe the right word is understanding—when it comes to how they feel. I don't want to scare ya away, but when I first met ya, then when we came together, even right now just laying here with ya, I feel a connection between us. It's unlike anything I have ever experienced in my life, Jennifer. I know this is where I need to be."

Rory spoke of his emotions with such conviction and certainty. He might joke around, but he didn't play games with people.

"I feel connected to you, too," she answered, putting her hand over his as he cupped her breast. She wondered if he could feel her heart beating beneath his palm. Her lids felt heavy as she tried to keep her eyes open. "I want to discuss this further, but after a double shift, poisoned cheese, fighting my inner demon in an effort not to kill you, being attacked by gremians, learning magic is real, and two really powerful orgasms, I don't think I can hold much more conversation."

"Of course, love, ya should rest." He stared at her as if he had no intention of closing his eyes. "I promise, no harm will come to ya within these walls."

"Could you get the lights?" she felt her eyes drifting closed.

The bed shifted slightly, and when she again

looked at him, the lights were off, and Rory had lit the fireplace. He hadn't moved from her side.

"Melt the blankets on top of me?" she mumbled, unsure if she made sense or not.

Rory chuckled. The bed again moved, and she felt him pulling the blanket from under her before he tucked her in manually.

"Doing that the human way was much less impressive than when you melted off my clothes," she mumbled, unable to look at him again.

Rory stroked her hair and kissed her cheek. "I'll show ya more magick in the morning. For now, ya rest..."

If he said more, she wasn't aware of it as she drifted off to sleep.

## Chapter Thirteen

Rory dozed but didn't fall into a deep sleep. Every time Jennifer moved or sighed, he felt compelled to check on her. It was his duty to protect her—not just because she was a woman and he a warlock, but because he was *her* warlock.

It wasn't duty that kept his mind awake and night crept through the window. He was afraid if he drifted into the land of dreams, he would return only to find Jennifer was just that—a dream.

When they touched, everything he wanted became apparent, as if her embrace had the power to pull him from a sleepwalking existence that he hadn't realized he was in. She was brightness and light and hope. She was his joy.

She was…his?

He prayed to any deity that would listen that she could be his, that this wasn't a fleeting moment in time but the first of many nights together. He hardly felt worthy of her, but that wouldn't keep him from wishing.

Rory had never wanted anything more in his life, and it had been a very long existence. At times he just floated through life. The span of a year rarely had meaning anymore. What was a month, a week, a day in comparison to forever? Decades had melted together, turning into centuries.

He didn't want this moment to slip away.

Rory placed his hand on Jennifer's side to feel her as his eyes refused to remain open. He detected the gentle rise and fall of her breath in a hypnotic rhythm.

It felt like only a second had passed, but his hand was flat on the sheet. He rubbed over the mattress as he pushed up to look for her. Jennifer was gone. Panic unfurled inside him.

"Jenn?" He pushed out of bed and hurried to the bathroom. "Jennifer?"

She wasn't there, but her work shirt was folded and draped over the side of the tub.

Rory put on his kilt and grabbed a fresh t-shirt before hurrying to go downstairs barefoot. There was any number of scenarios that could explain her absence, and none of them great—magickally possessed to retrieve an ancient blade to stab him with, kidnapped by his phoenix niece and forced to play princess tea party, tricked into accepting Raibeart's marriage proposal, sneaking out from a one-night stand.

Rory rushed down the stairs, unsure where he was going, but following his impulses as he turned toward the dining room. It was worse than anything he imagined.

His mother cornered Jennifer.

"Honestly, I'm torn. I need coffee, but I don't trust anything you hand me to consume," Jennifer was saying as he walked into the room. "Who knows what kind of acid trip awaits me in that brew?"

Both women turned to him at his entrance. Cait was dressed like a 1950s housewife ready to receive company. His ma held out an espresso mug toward Jennifer, who stared back at it with a dubious expression on her face.

Jennifer wore one of his black t-shirts and a pair of his plaid pajama pants rolled up at the ankles to turn them into capris. Her dark hair was a little messy from drying as she'd slept on it. Most women he'd known would feel at a disadvantage next to his very put-together mother, but Jennifer didn't appear to have such hang-ups.

"Rory, tell your lady friend that I am not trying to poison her," Cait said.

"Rory, tell your mother that I don't want to go on her magic carpet ride," Jennifer mimicked Cait's tone.

"Rory, tell your lady friend that I am not a murderess." Cait lifted the mug as if it were an affront to her honor that Jennifer would not take her at her word. "Or a drug dealer."

"Rory, tell your mother I want to see her drink it." Jennifer crossed her arms over her chest.

"I had my morning coffee," Cait stated, lowering the cup. "Another espresso, and I'll be jittery all day."

The last place Rory wanted to be was in the middle of an argument between his ma and his new girlfriend.

"How about I make ya a coffee?" Rory offered Jennifer.

Jennifer studied him for a moment and then looked pointedly at Cait. "Why don't you give it to your son to drink, then?"

Cait frowned.

"Sure, ma, I'll drink—" Rory began.

"I will not be thusly accused," Cait announced, taking the mug with her as she retreated to the kitchen in self-righteous anger.

"Oh my god," Jennifer said, pointing after

Cait as if the act of her leaving vindicated Jennifer in her suspicions. "She was trying to poison me again."

"Not poison," Rory said.

"You saw…"

"Probably just a little potion," Rory explained.

"Just a little potion? Like last night when I hallucinated that I was puking up clumps of smelly mud and leaking black fluid out of every orifice?" Jennifer shook her head. "I'm trying very hard to be understanding, Rory, because this magick thing is new to me, and I realize a lot is happening that I don't understand, but I cannot fathom why expelling mud is good for me."

"Who's expelling mud?" Iain came into the dining room on his way toward the kitchen.

"What are ya doing here?" Rory asked.

"Jane is worried about some of the plants in the back gardens. Something about a sinkhole?" Iain shrugged. "I told her she and the other ladies should jump in because it was probably one of those hot spring mud bath natural spa treatment things, but she didn't think I was amusing."

"That's because ya are not very funny," Rory said.

"At least I'm handsome," Iain quipped. "Unlike your unfortunate face—oh, hello, Jennifer."

Iain winked at her, pretending like he was just now seeing her.

"Hey," Jennifer answered.

"Ya want coffee? I was about to make some for Jane and me," he offered.

"No, thank you," Jennifer said. "And I recommend starting a fresh pot. Cait potioned the last one."

"She…" Iain quirked a brow and looked at Rory. "Potioned?"

"She knows about magick," Rory stated. "Our mothers gave her a crash course last night."

"Oh?" Iain glanced at Jennifer.

"Cheese ball," Jennifer said.

"I'm afraid to ask." Iain shook his head. "All I can say is, welcome to the asylum. Once you're in, you're never getting rid of us. Kind of like kudzu in the South."

Rory grimaced, expecting a bad reaction to Iain's joking.

Jennifer surprised him when she smiled. "Thank you."

Iain whistled as he continued to the kitchen. His voice could be heard coming from the other room. "Och, Aunt Cait, what is this I hear about ya giving Rory's girl a potion in a cheese ball?"

Jennifer walked around the table and came

toward him. She gave him a serious look and lowered her voice, "Can I ask you something?"

"Anything," he whispered.

"What in the world is kudzu?"

Rory chuckled. "It's an invasive plant that people say is slowly eating up the Southern landscape. Ya can see the vines draping over the trees when ya drive along the roads."

"Gotcha." She nodded.

"I didn't like waking without ya there next to me." Rory wasn't sure what prompted him to admit as much, but he didn't regret the words.

"I was going to bring coffee back for both of us, but your mother caught me going through the kitchen cabinets." Jennifer put her arms around his neck. "I wasn't snooping, I promise. I was looking for big coffee mugs. All I found were those tiny European espresso mugs, and that's not going to do it for my habit."

"I didn't assume ya were snooping," he said, wrapping his arms around her waist to keep her close to him. "Next time, wake me up, and I'll get it for ya."

"Next time?" She wrapped her arms a little tighter around him. "That's awfully presumptuous of you to assume, Mr. MacGregor. Though I will admit, I *was* snooping through your bedroom before I came down, making sure there were no pictures of old girlfriends hiding anywhere."

"Don't think I have any of those lying around, Miss, um…" Rory frowned. "Well, this is embarrassing, love."

"What?" She leaned back to study his face. Her arms slid from around his neck to rest on his chest. "You do have pictures of your exes? It's not a big deal. I was only teasing."

"No, not that. I'm afraid I don't know your last name." He heard footsteps coming down the stairs in the other room but didn't release her. It felt too good to hold her in his arms.

"To be fair, I did seduce you rather quickly," she said.

"Hey, I thought I seduced ya with my charms," he countered.

"Charm?" She tilted her head thoughtfully. "No, don't remember any charm. I do remember thinking your kilt was rather sexy. And we American girls are suckers for an accent."

"Are ya going to tell me your surname?" he asked.

"Haven't decided," she said, acting coy.

"What if I ask nicely?" He had to kiss her. How could he resist with her mouth being so close?

Jennifer gave a light moan as his lips moved against hers.

"Och, Raibeart! What in the name of all that is holy are ya wearing?" Murdoch's voice demanded from the kitchen. The elders typically stayed in the wing beyond the dining room and kitchen. It was evident the house was beginning to stir for the day.

"Ya like it? I ordered it online," Raibeart answered. "My package finally arrived."

"Oh, my stars!" Cait exclaimed.

"I like it, Uncle Raibeart," Iain said. "It's got…lots of holes."

"Ya can't wear that in public," Cait continued.

"First, I can't go naked. Now I can't wear clothes?" Raibeart cried in frustration. "Make up your bloody mind, woman!"

Jennifer pulled back from the kiss and laughed. "I'm sorry, I can't concentrate with all of them talking."

"Say the word, and I'll cast a spell to take away their voices," Rory offered.

"I kinda need to see what he's wearing." Jennifer tried to pull away to look.

"I need ya to tell me your last name," he said. "I can't go around saying you're my lady if I don't know at least that much. What will people think?"

Rory wasn't worried about what other people

thought of their relationship. Jennifer's opinion was all that mattered, but he did want to know everything about her.

"Maybe I'm a woman of mystery," she said.

"That ya are, love," Rory tried to pull her back into a kiss. He couldn't get enough of her.

"Greene," she whispered.

"Uh?" He arched a brow. "Yellow?"

"No, my last name is Greene," she said. "Jennifer Anne Greene. My mother tried to get people to call me Jenny Anne, but I hated that."

"Jennifer Greene." He frowned as he tried to place how he knew that name.

"It's not that bad." She hit his arm lightly.

"No, it's beautiful, like ya, but…" Rory loosened his hold. "Your name is Jennifer Greene?"

Why did he know that name?

"Are ya daft, laddie? I told ya she's a bog wench." Raibeart said. "Looks just like ole Jenny Greentooth, maybe a wee bit cleaner. No one ever listens to me."

Rory was about to scold his uncle when his gaze landed on Raibeart's crocheted overalls. The one-piece had straps on each shoulder and dipped low in the front to expose his naked chest with shorts that only came to mid-thigh. He didn't wear anything underneath. However, the most disarming part was the granny-square afghan pattern in brightly colored yarn.

Raibeart grinned at the attention and put his hands on his hips to pose. "Nice, huh? Margareta and Cait are always nagging me about losing my kilt, so I thought I'd add some variety to the wardrobe. Get with the modern times."

Raibeart turned to show the back, thrusting his hips back and forth as he moved his arms in stunted gestures that were probably meant to mimic a model.

"What do ya think? Fashionable, right?" Raibeart turned back around and lowered his voice in a whisper that wasn't all that quiet. "The best part is it's got these breeze holes, airy where a man needs to breathe."

"Ah," Jennifer made a weak noise.

"See, look at her, speechless." Raibeart winked. "Ladies can't resist a man who stands out. We're like peacocks that way."

Rory pried his eyes away and glanced down to where Jennifer stared as if frozen mid-word. He saw Raibeart give a few more poses out of the corner of his eye, and Rory lifted his hand to block the sight from Jennifer.

She pulled his hand down to unblock her vision. "Wait, did you just say I'm a...swamp hag?"

"Nae." Raibeart shook his head. "Bog hag."

"Bog wench," Rory quickly corrected, remembering the name Raibeart had said before his uncle's outfit had stunned all other thoughts from his mind. His modification hardly sounded better. "Uh, witch, wench, witch..."

None of it sounded flattering. This was bad.

Jenny Greentooth.

"Jennifer Greene. Jenny Greentooth. Jenny Greene. Jennifer Greentooth," Raibeart said, signing the words like a little ditty he had just made up.

"Oh, good, I'm a *bog witch* because that sounds so much better." Jennifer took a deep breath and looked back and forth between them. She pressed her hands to her mouth. "I don't even really know what a bog is. I mean, I know it's like a swamp in Scotland or something. And I heard of medieval bog people being found like mummies."

"Right, your old victims," Raibeart poked his fingers into some of the holes along the overalls waist like and wiggled the digits around like they came out his stomach. "Can't be too happy to have those lost souls found, eh?"

"I wasn't around in the medieval period," Jennifer stated.

"How was I to know your age?" Raibeart dismissed. "A gentleman knows better than to ask a lady about such a delicate thing." He wiggled his fingers faster. "Hey, Rory, check this out. It looks like I have ten little penis—"

"Stop!" Rory cut the man off.

"Don't be green with envy," Raibeart said, pulling his fingers from the holes. "Ha, Greene and green, what a pair."

"Ma, Raibeart is doing inappropriate things in front of Jennifer with the creepy baby jumper he's wearing," Rory called.

"Och!" Raibeart flinched and turned as he readied himself for Cait's wrath.

"Come on." Rory pulled Jennifer with him from the dining room. "We'll drive for coffee."

"We're not wearing shoes," she observed.

"Don't care. I need to get ya away from here before my family drives ya away for good." Rory was only half-joking. "I know they can be a lot."

"Bye, Jenny Greentooth!" Raibeart yelled. "Lovely to see ya again."

"Um, bye?" she mumbled.

Rory used his magick to open the front door.

"Is what he said...? Am I really an evil witch?" She started to turn back around as if to confront Raibeart.

"Allow me." Rory stopped her from returning to the dining room and lifted her into his arms. He cradled her as he carried her over the threshold and down the front steps toward his car. The cobblestone drive poked his feet, but he didn't care. "For the record, not all witches are evil. Like humans, many are good. It's all about choices."

If she turned out to be a witch, Rory didn't want her to have the wrong impression. He gestured the best he could and forced the car door to swing open without touching it. He sat her inside on the passenger seat.

"Front door." She pointed to where he'd left the door open. He waved his hand, and it slammed closed a little too loudly.

Rory ignored the giant gremian dents in his car as he went around to the driver's seat and got in. "Shall we make good our escape?"

"Yes, please," she said.

# Chapter Fourteen

Jennifer watched the trees pass by the window, happy to be running away from the mansion. As much as the MacGregors fascinated her—both as warlocks and as a close-knit family—they also overwhelmed her. Their energy was a bit much. Plus, she didn't trust the elders.

Jennifer touched her mouth, remembering the taste and texture of mud passing her lips.

Bog witch. How ridiculous was that idea? She wasn't any kind of witch, bog or not. Maybe she'd heard them wrong with the accent. Maybe Raibeart and Rory said grog wench, like an old term for a barmaid.

Maybe but doubtful. Jennifer wasn't about to start deluding herself now.

"I don't like people calling me Jenny," Jennifer

said, thinking of Raibeart's horrible nickname. She leaned her head against the glass and watched the side of the road as they turned out of the long driveway toward downtown. "My mom used to call me that."

"Used to? I'm sorry, did she pass away?" Rory's hand rested on her leg, drawing her attention from outside of the car.

"She walked out on us after my older brother died in a car accident. One of his friend's parents was driving. I don't think my mom could handle being around my dad and me after that. I heard her fighting with my dad once. She blamed his side of the family for cursing us with the worst luck." Jennifer sighed, unsure why she was telling him all of this. "The way she said it, too, like it was his fault."

Rory reached for her hand and held it as he drove.

"I think some people aren't meant to be parents," she said. "My dad was great, though."

"Was?"

"He died from cancer. Now it's just me. My dad didn't have any other family. And if my mom did, they never came around so I wouldn't know them." She took a deep breath. "I only remember pieces of her. I remember that her hands smelled like cigarettes when she touched my face before she left. It hurt at first. Then I was angry about it. Then something happened when I was taking care of my dad. I realized that her leaving was more about her deficiencies than it was about mine. I'm nothing like her. I don't run from hardship or responsibilities. It sucks, but that's what happened. I had an awesome dad to make up for her lacking."

*All it takes is a dash of destiny, and everything can change.*

Damn if her mother hadn't been right about that one.

"I can't imagine not having family," Rory said. "Iain's right, though. Once you're in our lives, we're like kudzu. There's no getting rid of us."

He turned the car into a parking lot and stopped in front of a small coffee shop.

"We're not wearing shoes, and I'm in pajamas," she said. "We can't go in there."

"I'm not having our second coffee date through a drive-thru like the first," he countered. "Ya wait here. I'll get it. What would ya like?"

"Can we count going to get fast food coffee last time as a date?" she asked, unable to help her smile.

"I am now that I know how low your former dates set the bar," he stated. "I mean, it's no hitting ya with my car, but—"

"Vanilla soy latte please," she interrupted.

"Done." He got out of the car.

"Oh, and a chocolate chip muffin?" she called after him.

He grinned, nodding. "Whatever ya wish, love."

Jennifer watched him through the window of the coffee shop. The barista giggled as she took his order, flinging her hair over her shoulder. Jennifer was more fascinated than jealous. Everyone Rory talked to walked away with a smile on their face. There was an easiness to his manner, and yet unmistakable confidence.

She leaned over to open the driver's side door when he returned with the coffees and a muffin. He handed her order to her.

"Shall we go somewhere to enjoy them?" he asked.

"Would you mind driving me home?" Jennifer held her latte in one hand and a giant muffin in the other. She leaned over to bite the top of the muffin while keeping the bottom wrapped in paper.

"Not at all." He put his coffee between his knees and pulled out of the parking lot.

"And would you mind going in with me?" she asked. "I know that weird voice I was hearing had something to do with—whatever that was."

"We'll call it a possession spell," he supplied.

"Yeah, that," she said. "I know that the voice wasn't real, but—"

"No, it was very real," he countered. "And, yes, I'll check your home for ya. Then, I think ya should pack a bag and stay with me."

"I don't think I can stay at the mansion," she said.

"Then at the motel with me," Rory stated. "I want to check on Jim anyway."

"Jim?"

"The puppy. I'm keeping him and naming him Jim."

Jennifer smiled. "That's nice to hear the little guy is getting a home. I've been a little worried about him."

"As I was saying, if ya don't want to stay in the mansion or the motel, I can take ya home, but I'll stay there with ya. Wherever ya are, I'm there too. I'm not leaving ya alone."

Jennifer could not see Rory MacGregor living in a trailer with her, not after seeing his mansion of a house.

"Don't you think I broke the spell or possession or whatever when I refused to stab you? The anger hasn't come back."

*All it takes is a dash of destiny, and everything can change.*

Rory grinned. "Glad to hear ya no longer want to stab me, but it's too soon to say whether or not it's over."

Rory drove toward her house. She had to stop him from going past it since the last time he'd dropped her off she hadn't shown in the actual location.

"Park here," she indicated, pointing to the curb.

He glanced at the two-story house near where she indicated. "It looks charming."

"I'm sure it is for the people who live there." Jennifer opened the car door and stepped onto the curb. She carried the latte and muffin with her. "Mine is this way."

Jennifer cut between the two houses toward the alleyway. She ate the muffin a little faster than in the car, letting crumbs fall on the ground. When they reached the trailer home, she frowned. "Crap. I think my key is back at the mansion."

Rory chuckled and lifted a finger. "Allow me."

He went to the latch and jiggled the handle. It opened.

"If this whole billionaire warlock thing doesn't work out for you, I think you have a real future as a locksmith." She hesitated as she glanced into the open doorway.

"It would have been more impressive if ya would have locked the door," Rory said.

Jennifer frowned. "Oh, yeah, I forgot. I ran out of here pretty quickly after hearing that creepy voice."

She remembered the money she'd left on the kitchen counter and hoped it was still there. If anyone tried the latch, she could have been out her tip money.

Rory went into the home and instantly began inspecting the rooms for an intruder. Jennifer went to the kitchen and grabbed the wad of cash that was thankfully still lying where she'd left it.

"All clear," Rory called.

"Thanks," she answered. "Uh, just have a seat in the living room if you like. I won't be but a minute."

His broader shoulders made the hallway leading past the bathroom feel small. Rory had to turn sideways to pass the washer. He went to sit on the couch.

Jennifer frowned as she opened the washer. The wet clothes left to sit overnight had a slight musty smell to them. The intruder had disrupted her routine, and she hadn't hung them over the shower rod to dry for her next shift.

"Do they have a laundry room at the motel for guests?" Jennifer asked.

"If they don't, I have magick," he answered.

Jennifer went to the bedroom to pack a duffel bag. She shoved all her cash and what little jewelry she had into the side pocket.

"Is this a picture of you with your dad?" Rory had found her one photo on the wall.

"Yeah, and my brother," Jennifer answered. She replaced his pajama pants with a pair of jeans and slipped on a pair of shoes. She put his pajamas in the bag to return later. "It's the only picture I have of us all together."

"You were an adorable child," he said.

In many ways, that photo was the most valuable thing she owned.

"Would you mind grabbing the picture for me?" she asked, setting her duffel bag on the counter and getting a small trash bag for her wet clothes. "I don't feel right leaving it here if I'm not going to be coming back each night."

"Anything else?" He brought the framed photo to her.

"No, that should about do it." She put the picture in the bag and zipped it. "I just need to get my work clothes."

"When is your next shift?" he asked. "I'll go in with ya."

At least he wasn't trying to tell her she couldn't work.

"Tomorrow," she answered. "That is if I still have a job after my performance last night. I was a freaking mess. I wouldn't blame the boss if he docks my pay for all the wrong orders that were sent back to the kitchen."

"Ya were not a mess. Ya were lovely," he said.

"Tell that to the lady who never got her margarita," Jennifer answered. She made sure to lock up as Rory carried her bags for her.

The ride to the motel was quiet. Jennifer drank her latte while worrying about how she'd apologize to Kay about dropping the ball.

At Hotel Motel, Maura appeared only too happy to put them in a room. She admitted that they were nowhere near capacity with the remodeling going on and had plenty of space. She gave them a room close to the parking lot so that they didn't have to carry their bags too far.

When Rory unlocked the motel room door for them, he instantly recoiled. This time, instead of cherub butts, the theme was clowns.

Nothing but pictures of happy smiling clowns, clown wallpaper, and carnival light fixtures. There was even a giant clown doll sitting in the middle of the bed.

"Oh, hell no, Bruce," Rory said, even though his twin wasn't there to hear it. He instantly pulled the door shut. "Wait here. I'll get us another room."

Rory ran back to the front office and returned minutes later with a key to the room next door.

"Apparently, Maura didn't know about the clown addition," Rory said. His movements were stiff, and he flinched a little as he opened the door to look inside. He let out a sigh of relief. "Oh, thank goodness. I'll take commercial banality over creepy circus any day. Sometimes Bruce is a little too artistically strange for his own good."

What the motel room lacked in character, it made up for in a fresh coat of paint and new carpeting. The pastel landscape on the wall of desert sands and cacti was borderline uninteresting. It matched the delicate pattern of the comforter and a chair next to a small table.

Jennifer found herself staring at the picture of the desert. Her vision blurred, and it looked as if the printed grains of sand were shifting and becoming darker. She blinked, but the idea remained, like a dream trying to peek through to reality.

"Jennifer?" Rory asked.

"What?" She forced her eyes away and found him next to the bathroom door staring at her.

Rory slowly came toward her. "How are ya feeling? Is the anger coming back?"

She shook her head. If anything, she felt sad. She never really talked about her mother and doing so had stirred a lot of feelings.

He lifted his thumb and brushed it across her cheek. She felt it slide in moisture. When he pulled it away, he showed her a dark tear staining his thumb.

Jennifer hurried into the bathroom to look into the mirror. Dark trails had leaked from her eyes down her face. She took several deep breaths, afraid to move in case the mud again filled her mouth. She lightly touched a tear and rubbed it between her fingers. There was a grainy texture to the moisture.

Rory appeared behind her in the mirror.

"I didn't want to believe you when you said the strangeness might come back. I hoped resisting the urge to kill you would have broken the spell." Jennifer grabbed a hand towel and wiped her face.

"Most spells and possessions are not easily broken. I'm not sure what this is." He touched her arm, and she pulled away from him.

Backing deeper into the bathroom, she faced him. "Rory, maybe you should not be around me."

Jennifer didn't want him to leave, but she was afraid of what might happen if he stayed.

"I don't know what I'm capable of and—" she tried to explain.

"I'm not afraid of ya, love. I know ya won't hurt me," he interrupted.

"I won't, but the spell might." Jennifer turned back to the mirror. She stared at her eyes, trying to see if something else lingered there. "Or the possession."

The idea of something living inside her terrified her.

"It's like I'm living a bad made-for-television movie," she whispered, pulling down her bottom eyelid to examine her eye more closely. "I have multiple personalities living inside me. When the alter takes over, I can't remember attacking you, except for the last time. Then I felt the outside will trying to force my hand."

"That might be because of the cheese," he said. "The potion was supposed to reveal the truth. I think that's what it did."

Jennifer didn't want to think about the tainted cheese ball.

A loud knock sounded on the door. Jennifer stiffened at the noise. She didn't want anyone to see her like this.

"It's probably Maura," he said. "I promise we're going to figure this out."

Jennifer nodded. She reached to shut the bathroom door behind him. "I just need a minute, and then I'll be out."

Rory leaned to kiss the back of her wrist as she held the knob. As if reading her deepest fear, he said reassuringly, "Ya are not alone, Jennifer. Ya have the whole of the MacGregor clan at your side. But, most importantly, ya have me. I'm not leaving ya."

"Thank you."

Jennifer closed the door behind him and turned to the mirror. She opened her mouth wide and tried to look into her throat. Then she held open her eyelids and studied each eye.

She heard muffled voices coming through the bathroom door. Maura and Bruce had joined them. A small bark followed their words.

Jennifer leaned her ear against the door to listen. She could barely make out what they were saying.

"Ma called. She's worried…" Bruce's voice sounded serious.

"…Jenny Greento…" Maura said.

"…bog…Ireland…can't…." Bruce added.

Jennifer quietly turned the handle and inched the door open, hoping they wouldn't notice and kept talking. She peeked out into the room through the narrow slit.

"I don't remember," Rory said.

"Sure ya do," Bruce said. "Ya were in Ireland, and ya followed a woman into a bog."

"No, I…" Rory gave a small laugh. "Oh, hey, little fella, easy there."

"Jennifer." Bruce smiled. "So good to see ya."

"Heard about ya trying to stab my brother," Maura said. "Can't say ya are the first to have had that impulse."

Jennifer knew they were trying to sound light-hearted, but their concern was evident in their eyes.

Rory held the black puppy she'd followed into the woods. The ball of fur struggled to be released. Rory obliged, and the scamp bounced playfully in her direction. His tag wagged so hard that it jerked his hips into the excited gesture.

"Oh, hey, hi, uh…" she greeted the dog.

"Jim," Rory supplied.

"Hi Jim," Jennifer finished, leaning over to pet the dog's head. He instantly tried to nip at her fingers.

"That's a stupid name for a dog," Maura said.

"Maura's a stupid name for a sister," Rory quipped.

"You're stupid," Maura taunted, mimicking a child.

"Ya are," Rory countered.

"Ya both are. Don't make me separate ya." Bruce grumbled as he moved to sit on the bed.

Maura stuck out her tongue and scrunched her nose.

Rory lifted his hand. This time his magick was yellow as he threatened his sister. "Don't make me freeze ya like that."

"Do, and I'll tell ma ya broke the rules," Maura answered. "They said no more petrifying spells. All ya boys up at the manor house couldn't handle your magick. They had to take it away from ya."

"Ya both realize Jennifer is witnessing this childish display." Bruce leaned against the head-board and folded his arms over his chest.

"By all means, continue." Jennifer stood. "I find it highly entertaining."

Rory's fingers grew brighter.

Maura held up her hand in warning. "No, don't!"

Rory laughed and extinguished the magick.

"Why did ya give them this serial killer suite?" Bruce looked around the room. "Ya know, just one door down, I just finished a new design."

Jennifer stiffened and looked around. "Serial killers stay here?"

"He's joking," Maura dismissed before turning a pointed stare at Bruce. "Ya are joking, right? Ya haven't hidden weapons or body parts in the walls or anything creepy like that?"

"No body parts," Bruce answered. "Ya know how the neighbors of the killer are always interviewed afterward, and they talk about how normal and boring the guy was? That's what this room is. Normal and boring. But if ya look at it, it's a little too normal and too boring, like it's trying too hard to convince us it's not what it really is."

"They do say it's the quiet ones you have to look out for," Jennifer agreed. "Maybe it's the quiet rooms you have to be wary of, too."

"Exactly!" Bruce pointed at her. "Thank ya, Jennifer. It's nice to have someone with a brain to talk to."

"Well, I'm not putting serial killer suite on the brochures," Maura said. "In fact, I'm regretting going into business with ya on this place."

"That's because ya lack vision," Bruce answered, unconcerned.

"And ya lack business sense. This is Green Vallis, Wisconsin, not a Hitchcock movie." Maura turned to Jennifer, effectively ending the conversation with her brother by asking, "How are ya feeling, Jennifer? Ma said ya had a bit of spell."

"I'm *under* a spell," she corrected. "Or possessed with like a demon or something."

"What?" Maura looked between her two brothers. "I thought they said Jenny Greentooth. No one mentioned we were dealing with a demon—"

"No," Rory interrupted. "Not a demon."

All Jennifer got out of that little exchange was that actual demons were real. She hugged her arms against her stomach and tried not to think about it.

"Bog witch," Rory picked Jim up off the floor and then sat on the end of the bed near his brother's feet. He released the puppy to play on the mattress.

"Oh, well, at least that's something." Maura sat down in the pastel chair next to the table. "I can't handle another apocalyptic battle. I don't remember the bog witches ever wanting to take over the world, just collect a few souls."

"How did ya escape the bog witch when ya were in Ireland?" Bruce asked.

Rory averted his eyes.

Jim started digging at the comforter, trying to bunch it up. He walked in a tight circle several times before plopping down in the nest he'd tried to make for himself.

"Tell me ya didn't seduce her." Maura silently gagged. She held up her hand toward Jennifer. "Sorry. I know the two of ya are…something."

"In love," Rory answered.

Jennifer's mouth opened in surprise at how easily he claimed to be in love with her.

"Uh, I think maybe that's a conversation ya should have with your girlfriend when we're not around. It seems to be news to her," Bruce said.

Rory looked at her and gave a light shrug. "I'm not ashamed of my feelings."

"I…" Jennifer wasn't used to talking about these things, especially not in front of an audience. Jim was the only one in the room not staring at her. She slowly sat on the foot of the bed, bending one leg so she could face them while keeping one foot on the floor. "I want to know what happened with the bog witch in Ireland."

"It was what…?" Rory looked at his brother.

"Mid-1600s, maybe?" Bruce guessed.

"Aye, something like that." Rory sighed. "I can't recall how I escaped. I remember seeing someone who I thought needed help. She lured me into the bog. Or maybe I'm remembering stories I've heard told over the years. It all happened such a long time ago."

*Four hundred years ago.*

Jennifer looked at Rory anew, studying his face.

Maura laughed. "Look, she's calculating how old ya are."

"No, I…" Jennifer chuckled. "Yeah, I was."

"A woman lured ya into the bog," Bruce prompted his twin to keep telling his story.

"I must have been stuck at that point. I'm guessing my magick didn't work to get me out of there and…" Rory scrunched up his face.

"Remember." Maura gestured to her brother with both hands. A light pink trailed from her fingers like smoke-snakes.

The trails entered into Rory's eyes. He inhaled sharply.

"Aye, I was stuck in an enchanted bog. My magick wouldn't work, and I couldn't save the woman I followed," he said, his accent becoming a little thicker. "A child circled me, not falling in, and then pushed me deeper so that I was trapped."

Rory rubbed his eyes and shook his head.

"A child?" Bruce frowned.

"From a nearby village, maybe?" Rory stroked Jim's head. "The rest of the memory is blank. Though, it does make sense in a way. Each time Jennifer has been compelled to harm me, I've been restrained and without magick. It's that same trapped feeling. Plus, she comes after me with an ancient blade from that part of the world. No matter how many times we lock it in the vault, the weapon finds its way back to her like it belongs to her."

"It's not much, but it's a start." Maura pushed up from the chair. "I'm going to go to the office and call Ma. I'll tell her what ya told me. She'll probably want ya back at the house."

"I'm not going up there," Jennifer denied. "Not after that cheese."

"Cheese?" Maura frowned. "Did Ma…?"

"No. She didn't try to human cook," Rory answered. "She laced a cheese ball with some kind of discovery potion, and Jennifer reacted with hallucinations—"

"It was like being on an acid trip," Jennifer put forth. "A bad one, too. Instead of unicorns and bunnies, I choked out balls of mud and cried dirty water."

"I've never seen unicorns when I was on acid," Bruce mused. "Though I did see a herd of albino buffalos chasing a naked leprechaun."

Rory and Maura turned to look at their brother.

"It was the sixties. I'm an artist. Free love and all that," Bruce said. "Not to dismiss what ya were telling us, Jennifer. I'm sorry my ma slipped a spell on ya."

"Just when we think the elders are finally catching up with the times, they pull some of that authoritarian medieval magick crap," Maura grumbled.

"For the good of the family," Bruce said with an exaggerated tip of his head.

Jennifer couldn't tell whether or not he believed the words.

"Keep the family secret at all costs. Mortals can't know about magick. They can't handle the truth. Take their memories." Maura waved her hands as if she could erase all she just said. "Ugh. Just ugh. I don't know how ya stay around all that, Rory. I wouldn't move back into the family home if ya promised me a thousand granted wishes."

"Because they're family," Rory said. "I know ya have had your issue with some of the old ways, but family is family. We're always there for ya if ya like it or not."

Jennifer stared at her trembling hands. She didn't have that. There was no family safety net waiting for her with open arms to help her through this bog witch thing.

"Ya would take issue with the old ways too if ya were a lady," Maura said. "Ask our cousin. She knows. Why do ya think Malina ran off to live in Vegas with a luck demon? It's not easy being a young MacGregor woman."

Jennifer coughed to hide her sudden laugh at Maura's use of the word young. Considering most of them were hundreds of years old, it's not a word that would apply.

"Ya all right, love?" Rory asked.

"Just a little dust," Jennifer dismissed.

"The men acting like we're delicate flowers to be protected," Maura continued, ignoring the interruption. "Our mothers telling us to act like ladies with pearls and white gloves so that it's impossible to throw a proper fireball at a troll horde. Have ya ever tried to hold magick through dainty white gloves? Bloody things stain so badly. And forget running when your corset is laced so tight—"

"Tirade, sister," Bruce interrupted.

"Aye, wee rant," Rory agreed, his attention more on the puppy than his sister.

"Well, it sucks is all I'm saying," Maura finished.

"Stepping away from my sister's seventeenth-century undergarment trauma for a moment," Bruce said. "Jennifer, I welcome ya to stay at this motel as long as ya like, especially until we get this bog witch mystery figured out."

"Thank you," she answered.

"I'm staying too," Rory said. "And Jim."

"Maura, how about I call ma to tell her what's happening, and ya can go to the grocery store and pick up provisions," Bruce suggested.

"Why do I have to do the shopping?" Maura crossed her arms over her chest.

"Aye, ya are woman, and I hear ya roaring or whatever, but do we want me in the lady parts aisle getting the feminine whatnots?" Bruce asked. "Or do ya think maybe this once ya can do the shopping?"

"This may be wrong, but I kind of want to see what feminine whatnots your brother things I need," Jennifer whispered to Rory.

It wasn't quiet enough because they all started laughing.

"I'm a little curious too, Bruce. What whatnots does a lady need?" Maura asked.

"Ya know, those little cotton missile launchers and lily of the valley powder." Bruce made a gesture as if to mimic a woman patting body powder on her cleavage. "Toiletries. Lady whatnots."

"So tampons and perfumed body powder," Maura stated. "Those are the emergency supplies that ya think a lady needs?"

"Aye, *tampion*," Bruce said.

"Tam-pon," Maura sounded out.

"Aye, *tampion*," Bruce repeated.

"A *tampion* is a plug ya put in front of a gun muzzle, ya halfwit," Maura said. "This isn't medieval France."

"He's messing with ya, Maura," Rory said.

"Point made. I'll do the shopping," Maura walked toward the door and pulled it open, getting ready to leave. "Jennifer, make a list, and I'll get ya whatever ya need later. For now, I'll pick up something for lunch and a bunch of snacks for the room."

"And for ya, my dear sister," Bruce added, jumping up from the bed to follow her, "don't forget to pick up your smelling salts. I would hate for ya to have a fainting fit, ya delicate flower."

The door shut behind them.

Now that they were alone, Jennifer said. "They're sweet, your siblings."

"Aye." Rory nodded.

"And very generous." She crawled toward the head of the bed to take over Bruce's spot.

"Aye." Rory grinned. "They like ya. I can tell."

"So," Jennifer glanced around the motel room. "You, me, and Jim on a Green Vallis motel vacation. I suppose I can think of worse ways to spend our time."

"If ya don't want to be here, I'll take ya wherever ya want to go. The mansion, your home, Edinburgh. Do ya want to go to Edinburgh?"

"Well, yeah, of course I do. Who doesn't want to go to Scotland?" she asked. "But I think here is probably the best plan for now. At least until I stop trying to kill you."

"Whatever my lady wishes," Rory said. The puppy attacked his hand, and he laughed. "Isn't that right, Jim? Jennifer can have whatever her heart desires."

"He's an unusual dog, isn't he? What kind do you think he is?" she asked.

"Cute." Rory shrugged.

"I meant the breed," Jennifer clarified.

"Maura took him by the vet. They think he's a schipperke and possibly part something else."

"Schipperke? I've never heard of that kind," she said. "His face looks kind of like a miniature bear cub."

"They make great watchdogs and were used to catch rats around barges," he said.

"Interesting." She petted Jim's head. "Did you have to look that up?"

"Told ya we like animals," he said. "I've been around a while."

"Why don't you let Jim play on the floor? Then make sure that door's locked and come here, Mr. MacGregor?" Jennifer grinned. "I can think of one thing this lady desires."

Rory shot a stream of magick at the door. The lock chain moved on its own, sliding into place.

He leaned over the side of the bed to gently lower Jim to the floor.

Rory crawled toward her. His clothes dropped off his body without effort. When he reached her, he was completely naked.

"What were ya saying, love?" Rory kissed the corner of her mouth. "I am here to serve."

## Chapter Fifteen

Being stuck in a room for a day and a half with Rory was as close to perfect as she would ever find, and thanks to his magickal abilities, quickly dressing when his siblings came to the door was literally a breeze. Their clothes blew onto them with a magickal whirl...and then back off again when they were alone.

Actually, every second with Rory could be considered a magickal whirl.

A beautiful dash of destiny.

"What are ya thinking just now?" Rory whispered against her temple. His hand rested across her naked waist. An occasional tingle vibrated her skin where they touched as if his magick flowed just beneath his surface.

The sound of murmuring voices came from

the television, but they'd stopped paying attention to the show. They heard Jim's paws running playfully around on the floor. The dog was obsessed with a squeaky hamburger toy Bruce had brought him.

"All it takes is a dash of destiny, and everything can change," she answered.

Rory chuckled.

She leaned back to study him. "What?"

"That's rather deep thinking," he said. "You're being philosophical, and I was thinking about… now I'm not sure I want to say."

"Now you have to say," she skated her fingertips along his arm, drawing aimless patterns.

He grinned. "How beautiful your arse is."

Jennifer laughed. "Your *arse* isn't too bad, either."

"I like that phrasing." He kissed her neck. "All it takes is a dash of destiny."

"It was the last thing my mother said to me," she admitted. "Though, I don't want to talk about her right now when we're lying here like this."

"Do ya want your clothes?" he offered.

"I want your kisses before I have to get up and get ready for my shift," she said.

"Gladly." Rory leaned over and kissed her.

Jennifer reached for his face. She intended to keep him close, but her fist clenched.

"Oh, ow, love, that—" Rory reached toward where her hand pulled his hair.

Her hand shook, and a white heat ran down her arm. When it hit her shoulder, the sensation exploded into her body in liquid hot rage.

Jim began barking, the high-pitched yelp sounding distressed.

"There you are," she ground out, unable to stop the words.

An outside force took over her body, causing her limbs to spasm. Jennifer kept hold of him as her free hand slapped against the mattress. Her fingers splayed, searching.

"Jennifer? Love, it's me. Rory. Ya don't want to do this." He dug his hands underneath her grip on his hair and tried to pry them away from his head.

"There you are," she said through clenched teeth. This was not what she wanted to say. This was not what she wanted to do.

"Jennifer, please," Rory begged.

Jim barked louder.

"Hey, is everything all right?" Maura yelled as pounding started on the door.

Bruce and Maura charged into the room.

"Jennifer, no!" Maura shouted.

A yellow light flashed. Jennifer's body began to stiffen.

"There you—"

---

"Ow," Rory grunted.

Jennifer became as hard as a statue beneath him at the petrifying spell his sister cast to stop the attack. Her fist still gripped his hair.

"Please tell me you're not naked under those covers," Maura said.

"Aye," Rory answered, trying to pry himself free. "A little help here."

"Maura, get scissors," Bruce instructed.

"Aye," Maura answered. Rory heard her footsteps hurrying from the room.

Rory braced his weight and called forth his magick to clothe Jennifer's statuesque form. His energy was weak, but at least it worked now that she was immobilized. The second that she'd attacked, he had been unable to fight her.

"So, what did ya do?" Bruce appeared next to the bed holding Jim.

"It's the spell. It traps me and leaves me helpless to…" Rory grumbled, trying to pull the hair from his head to break free. Jennifer's face was trapped with a snarling expression. Her eyes were narrowed as if they still stared at him, but he knew she couldn't see in her current state.

"Helpless to?" Bruce prompted. "I didn't quite catch that last part."

"Helpless so she can stab me with a knife," he answered.

"Knife?" Bruce walked around to the other side of the bed. "Oh, what do ya know. She's holding a knife. When Maura comes with the scissors, I wouldn't move around too much. Ya might stab yourself in the side."

Maura rushed back into the room. "Don't move, Rory."

"Oh, aye, I was just about to pop out for a movie," Rory answered.

"Don't take your bad mood out on me," Maura said.

"Oh, wait," Bruce said, grabbing their sister's arm as she tried to lean onto the bed. He took out his phone and snapped a picture.

"Dammit, Bruce," Rory jerked his head to no avail. "This isn't a joke."

"No, but it is kind of funny," Maura said. "Send me a copy."

"This will be my entry for the family Christmas card this year," Bruce said. "Unless she kills ya. Then it would be in bad taste."

"Hold still," Maura instructed. "I don't want to cut ya."

He heard the scissors slicing through his hair

as the grip on his head eased.

"Careful, there's a knife near your side," Maura said as she cut the last of his trapped hair. He sat back slowly, barely missing the blade Jennifer wielded toward him.

"I'd be happy to teach ya about pleasing a woman," Bruce offered with a snicker. "Ya know, so this kind of thing doesn't happen again."

"This isn't funny," Rory stated.

"No, it wouldn't be funny if she stabbed ya. As it is, she merely tried to stab ya, and that's a bit funny," Bruce countered.

Rory saw his kilt on the floor and gestured toward it with his hand, magickally dressing before he came from under the covers.

"She looks…" Maura angled her head and studied Jennifer. "Outraged."

"Aye." Rory rubbed his sore head, feeling the uneven locks. He didn't care that they were cut.

*There you are.*

He couldn't get that creepy voice out of his mind.

"This is too close," Maura said. "I know ya wanted to stay here to make sure she was better, but this isn't better. She came close to succeeding in her mission."

"It's not her mission. She's under a spell," Rory denied. Even as he said it, he stared at the blade. A few seconds more and he would've been impaled upon it. "This isn't Jennifer's doing. She's being used."

"Regardless, ya know we need the help of the others on this," Bruce said.

"She doesn't want to go to the mansion." Rory sat on the bed next to her and touched her stony face.

"I understand that ya want to honor her wishes, but it's no longer her call to make." Maura patted his shoulder. "It's time we took her to the mansion. Look at her face, Rory. See for yourself how strong this spell is."

Rory stroked Jennifer's face. He didn't want these days sequestered with her to end, but as he looked into her angry, statue eyes, he knew that it was already over.

"I love her," Rory said.

"We know." Maura touched Jennifer's fist where soft strands of Rory's hair still splayed from between her fingers.

"I don't want to be without her. Even if it means she'll kill me," Rory said. "If I have to die—"

"How about we leave the dramatics of star-crossed lovers for Shakespeare?" Bruce interrupted. He still held Jim. "We can put her in the back of the truck. I have a tarp and some tie-downs. Everyone will think we're transporting a Greek statue."

"Good idea," Maura said.

"Wait—" Rory frowned. "She's not furniture."

"Do ya have a better idea? She'll weigh a ton in this state, and we can't exactly bend her knees to make her sit in your car." Bruce arched a brow as he awaited an answer that didn't come. "I'll pull around front. Try to get her ready to transport."

Bruce left the room carrying Jim.

"I'll call ma and let her know we're coming," Maura said. "We should try to get that knife out her hand before she thaws."

## Chapter Sixteen

Jennifer felt heavy. She couldn't lift her arms or legs. Her vision was blurred, and though she was sure she blinked, she couldn't detect the gentle pressure. Patterns of light shifted and moved in front of her, but she couldn't make out the exact shapes.

"I think she's coming to." Cait MacGregor's voice was the last thing Jennifer wanted to hear.

Had they drugged her again?

Were her lungs taking in air?

Why couldn't she move?

She started to panic. What kind of new hell was this?

Someone pried at her hand.

"Got it," Cait said. "Angus could you put this horrible knife somewhere, anywhere? Maybe take it through the mirror portal to Erik's house and tell him to keep an eye on it for us. The vault isn't working, and we need to keep it away from her if possible."

"Aye. Margareta is already there visiting Lydia," Angus answered. "They say they're coming up with tea blends, but I know they're playing with potions."

"Better not be love potions. I can't handle more of Erik's singing," Euann said.

The blurry shadows moved, but Jennifer couldn't turn her head to watch them. However, she could follow what they were saying, but she knew there was more to the story she didn't understand—mirror portals and love potions?

"Do ya think she can hear us?" Euann asked.

*Yes. Yes, I can hear you.*

A steady rhythm bumped against her shoulder several times.

"Hey, stop that," Rory ordered.

"She looks angry," Euann observed. "I almost don't recognize her with that expression."

*Rory? What's happening? What's wrong with me?*

"Is that our Jenny Greentooth?" Raibeart's voice sounded far away. "Looks like she put on a little weight."

*Hey!*

Well, they had been eating a lot of fast food lately, but still…

"Ya better be careful, brother," Murdoch said. "This lassie knows how to wield a knife."

"Petrifying spells tend to add a few hundred pounds," Bruce said. "We had to haul her in the back of my truck just to get her here."

She again had the vague impression that someone touched her, this time patting her head.

*Hello. I'm right here. Why is everyone talking around me?*

They didn't answer. Jennifer hated this. She felt as if she screamed through a fog.

*Am I dead?*

"Don't ya listen to him, Jennifer," Murdoch said. "Ya are lovely."

*No. No, that can't be it. They're not talking like I'm dead.*

*Hello? Rory? Rory, can you hear me?*

"Stop looking at me like that, ma. I know you're stupid rule about not petrifying each other, but I had to do something," Maura said.

*Petrify? Like fossilized wood or something? Is that what happened?*

"She was going to stab Rory," Maura continued.

"We were lucky to get there in time to stop

her," Bruce added. "Thanks to Maura's quick thinking."

*Oh, crap. Did I try to kill Rory again?*

Jennifer remembered being in bed with him, kissing him.

*Hear me, Rory. Hear me. Connect with my mind.*

Jennifer didn't expect her mind-meld experiment to work, but hey, it was worth a try. She concentrated on projecting her thoughts to him.

*Rory. Rory. Rory.*

"What happened to your crocheted jumper monstrosity?" Rory asked.

"Och, don't mention that devil's garment! It might have looked good, but after a time, the breeze holes weren't so breezy," Raibeart said. "Yarn against the man-baubles is not an inspired idea. They're meant to be flashed, not chafed."

"Is that why you're walking like ya just hopped off the back of a horse?" Euann teased.

"Green Vallis is a respectable place," Cait insisted, "not a nudist colony. Naked runs in the forest are one thing, but ya cannot keep going into town without clothes."

"I don't know. I think some of the locals could use a little naked time," Maura put forth wryly.

Laughter met her statement, but somehow, even without being able to see, Jennifer guessed Cait wasn't one of those laughing.

"Just yesterday, we had this woman pretending to be interested in renting rooms by the hour," Maura continued, "but it was more like she wanted me to admit we would do it. She kept winking at me. It was unsettling."

"About this tall, short gray hair, and a pencil tucked behind her ear?" Euann asked.

"Yes," Bruce answered. "That's her."

*Callister. It's Callister.*

"Mrs. Callister," Euann stated.

*I knew it!*

It was like she was a child, and Jennifer had to be quiet while the adults talked over her. She found it annoying.

"Mrs. Callister thinks she's a journalist. She has a gossip blog and likes to make up lies about people," Euann said. "I bet ya a hundred dollars she's about to post a story about the prostitution ring you're running out of the motel."

"Ah, and I wanted that guest services' feature to be a surprise," Maura pouted.

A choking noise sounded.

"Ma, that was a joke," Maura said.

"Ya were not blessed with humor," Cait stated.

"Raibeart, why don't ya take one for the town and go ask that Mrs. Callister if she'll marry ya," Rory asked. "Keep her busy and off the internet. Jennifer said she's been posting lies about them as well, implying they take men to the back room during their shifts."

"That's one woman I don't want saying aye to my proposal," Raibeart answered. "If that is who my friend Fate had in mind, I'll throw that miserable fish back into the ocean."

"What is her obsession with prostitution?" Euann wondered aloud.

"What are ya grumbling about?" Rory asked. "She has a crush on ya, and only writes nice flowery poetry about her sweet Euann. What did she call ya? A breath of fresh Scottish air? A kilted example of masculinity?"

"Not since I married Cora," Euann said. "Now, I might be a pickpocket."

*Hey, guys, anyone want to tell me how long I'm going to be stuck like this?*

Jennifer hated this. All she had was her blurry vision and the sound of their voices moving around her.

"Ya should let me fix that haircut while we're waiting," Cait said. "Ya look like your sister hacked ya with a chainsaw."

"Stop fussing. It's fine, Ma," Rory dismissed. "I don't care about my hair. We need to focus on breaking Jennifer's enchantment the second this petrifying spell wears off."

"He's right, Ma," Bruce said. "We can all see she loves Rory."

"Aye," Maura agreed. "Until the enchantment takes over. Then she wants to kill him."

"Some would say that's how true love works," Murdoch joked.

*That's not fair. I didn't say that yet. I mean, yes, sure, I have feelings for him. Yes, I probably do love him, which kind of scares me. And he did tell his siblings he loved me, but we haven't had that talk. It's not a talk I want to include his poisonous mother on. Rory and I are still getting to know each other. We're still in the fun sex phase of things. I mean, have ya see Rory naked? It's a little hard to think of anything else.*

"Oh, aye, lassie, I have seen Rory naked," Raibeart said. She felt another pat on her shoulder. "He is an unfortunate looking lad, but ya have a good heart to love him like ya do."

*Wait. What? Did you hear that, Raibeart?*

"Of course I heard that," Raibeart answered.

"Heard what?" Rory asked. "Who's unfortunate looking?"

"Raibeart?" Cait insisted.

*What's happening to me?* Jennifer thought.

"I'm talking to Jennifer," Raibeart said. "Someone should. Ya have all been ignoring her."

"Ya can hear her?" Rory asked. "What's she

225

saying? Is she angry? Is she in pain? Is she scared?"

"Ya can't hear her?" Raibeart asked.

"What's she saying?" Rory insisted.

"She's thinking of your naked arse," Raibeart answered.

*I didn't say that!*

"She says mine is better," Raibeart continued. "And she says she's been seriously considering my marriage proposal."

*What? No, I—*

"He can't hear her," Rory dismissed. "She would never say that."

*Raibeart, tell them you can hear me!*

"I can hear her," Raibeart said, "and she has a thing for me, as all the ladies do. Obviously, we're connected."

*No, tell them you can hear me for real.*

"For real," Raibeart added.

"Do ya need to be here?" Rory asked his uncle. "This is serious."

*No, don't go. I'm scared. Tell Rory I'm afraid. How long will I be like this?*

"Laddie can't take a joke," Raibeart said, and she felt that he'd leaned closer to her.

*Tell—*

"Oh, aye, Jenny, I'll tell them. I can hear her. She's in love with ya, but she's confused like most bog wenches. I think it's all that time they spend suspended in the muck. Unlucky lot. Tend to go mad. Touched in the head, but it can't be helped." Raibeart chuckled. "She doesn't care for ya much, Cait."

*What? No, don't say that!* Jennifer continued trying to mind-tell him to shut up even as he kept talking.

"I think she's plotting against ya cause she doesn't want me to tell ya she called ya a poisonous—what did ya call her? I'm having a little trouble with all the yelling."

"Jennifer, love, if ya can hear me, everything is going to be all right. We're back at the MacGregor home. Maura put ya in this state so we could stop the enchantment from killing me. It will wear off, and ya will be fine, I promise. But, for now, I think we need to stay here until the next episode hits."

"Jennifer, it's Cait," Rory's mother spoke loudly next to Jennifer's face. "I did not try to poison ya. That was a small potion to bring out the truth so that we could help ya."

"Don't lie to her, Ma," Maura said. "Ya did it to help Rory, not Jennifer. She deserves to hear the truth."

"Help both of them," Cait said, only to add louder, "Jennifer, I did it to help both of ya. I didn't know it would bring the truth out in such literal terms. Choking on peat is very telling, though. It means ya have the bog witch inside ya, affecting ya."

"Women like to be called wenches, not witches," Raibeart stated. "Unless they are a witch, then it's all right. It's called political correctness, Cait."

"That's not how that works," Bruce said. Everyone ignored him.

Cait continued in her loud tone, "Since ya have been at the motel, I've been brewing up another batch. The cheese ball contained the last of my stock. I think if ya tried it again, we might learn more."

*Oh, hell no. You keep your potions away from me, devil woman.*

"She'll think about it," Raibeart said.

"Good," Cait answered. "I'm happy to hear you're being reasonable."

*Please tell her she doesn't need to yell. I can hear her.*

Before Raibeart got the chance to mess up that message too, Rory said, "Ma, please go check on the potion and make sure it's ready if Jennifer wants to try it—but only if she wants to. Bruce, can ya take Jim outside for a bit and feed him?"

"Aye," Bruce said. "Come on then, Jim."

"Careful, there have been gremians in the area

again," Murdoch said. "They should be sleeping this time of day, but they'll try to ride Jim like a pony if they run across him."

"Oh, aye, those hellions have been hunting me," Raibeart said. "Little do they know it's a trap, and I'm hunting them."

"I'll help with the potion," Maura said. "I have a cut on my leg I need ya to look at anyway, Ma. It's not healing fast enough."

"I'm staying here until Jennifer comes out of this petrified state," Rory said.

"Come, Raibeart, let's leave the love birds alone," Murdoch said. "I think I heard Jewel playing dragon slayer upstairs. We should probably make sure she doesn't conjure an actual dragon."

"I taught her that one," Raibeart answered proudly. "Being a pretty princess and drinking tea is all well in good, but my little phoenix is also going to learn how to kick arse."

"I'll be sure to tell Kenneth ya are the one to get credit for it," Murdoch answered.

"No one is ever going to hurt that wee bairn," Raibeart insisted.

"Oh, love," Rory whispered next to her. "I wish I could hear ya. Don't read anything into the fact that I can't. Uncle Raibeart is a special kind of touched. He tends to see beyond the veil more than the rest of us."

*I wish you could hear me too.*

"I promise I won't leave your side," Rory said. "And, since this is going to be a one-way conversation, I'll try to make it entertaining. I'm also only going to tell ya stories where I end up looking good. I have to impress my lady, after all."

*I'm already impressed. Thank you for not leaving me alone.*

Rory cleared his throat. "Have ya ever heard of the fine sport of caber tossing?"

# Chapter Seventeen

Jim bounced across the back garden, running in circles as he chased leaves. The puppy didn't have a care in the world. Jennifer sat with Rory on a stone bench, watching Jim scamper from the cobblestone path into the thick grass lining it. The dog didn't venture toward the trees, which was good since she didn't want to chase him through the woods again. She was a little jealous of his innocence.

Jennifer rubbed her arms, reassuring herself that she was pliable. Being stuck in a stone-cast state had been a horrible feeling. She could hear and think, but her body had been imprisoned. Though it felt like days, Rory assured her it had been mere hours.

Rory had stayed beside her, mostly talking

about sports and old mischiefs the family had found themselves in. At the end of each story, he would give a small laugh and announce that he was the one who'd saved the day. Usually, his two cousins Iain and Euann would come out looking like idiots.

Rory's interpretation of the past was clearly self-biased.

She didn't care. He'd kept his word, and she had been very entertained while she'd softened.

"Hey, guys!" Maura appeared around the side of the house. "I got your contraband."

Jennifer laughed as Maura tossed a to-go bag from a local sandwich shop at them. Rory caught it with one hand, keeping his other around Jennifer's shoulders.

"Much obliged," Rory said.

"No worries," Maura answered, barely breaking stride as she reversed her steps. "I wouldn't trust anything that came out of Ma's kitchen right now either. I have to get back before she starts wondering where I ran off to. She's a little on edge thinking one of her baby boys is in trouble."

"What about the Crimson Tavern?" Jennifer asked.

"I called your boss and let him know ya weren't coming in. I lied and told him ya were sick. I know how important the job is to ya." Maura gave a small wave before turning to jog toward the back door.

"I hope I'm not fired after this," Jennifer said. Having someone call in for her wasn't the most professional way to handle a job. It's not like she was in a coma. "I wouldn't blame him after my performance the other night."

"Ya can't dwell on that," Rory said. "It wasn't as bad as ya fear."

"That's sweet, but it was," she said.

"If he does fire ya, we'll find ya another job." Rory grinned. "And ya do know ya are dating a rich—"

"I'll stop you right there," Jennifer said. "I've always earned my way. I'm not with you because you have money. I don't need you to start paying my rent like a sugar daddy."

Rory set the food bag on his lap and opened it with one hand. He handed her a sandwich. "Hey, look, see, they've stopped staring at us."

Jennifer glanced back to the window. Their chaperone was gone.

"Thank you for not making me eat your mother's potion." Jennifer peeked between the bread. "I know they think it will help, but…"

Jennifer sighed and took a bite of the sandwich. Thawing from a petrifying spell had left her famished.

Rory pulled her closer, keeping the hand draped around her shoulders. He ignored his sandwich, more concerned with holding her. "My ma doesn't know how to be helpless. The truth is, she doesn't know what is causing this enchantment. So she hopes by forcing truths out of ya, she'll figure out the answer. I'll let her brew her potion because it will keep her busy."

Jim found a particularly fascinating leaf and brought his shoulders low to the ground as he waited for it to move. His back legs were straight, keeping his bum in the air. His tail wagged erratically. Damn, he was cute. And so small.

"And you? What do you think?" She took another bite.

"I think that these webs have to untangle on their own. There will be an answer, but magick has a way of revealing itself. We just have to wait, watch, and be vigilant."

Jennifer turned in her seat to look toward the back of the house. The shrubs were manicured and spaced with precision, and not a single weed grew between them. A shadowed figure peered out at them from a window. She couldn't tell which uncle it was, but the man lifted his hand at her attention to show he was avidly watching.

"I think the watching part is taken care of," she said, waving back.

"It won't be like this for long," he assured her.

"No? How long do these enchantment-possession-spell things usually last?" She wondered if he was just trying to make her feel better.

"Depends. From start to finish? Some are in the making for centuries. Others are ten, twelve years. Some are short, fast, like a blow to the gut, but then over."

"How long from the time they activate until they are done?" she clarified.

Centuries? Her definition of not long was more like half a day. Being mortal with less than a hundred years lifespan probably did put things like time in a different perspective. Also, her sense of urgency would be a little higher, considering she'd never dealt with the supernatural before.

"Months at best," he answered.

"And at worst?"

He bit his lip, mumbling, "Centuries."

"Centuries." She leaned away from him to study his face.

"But customarily that's a sleeping curse or being encased in stone or turned to salt or—"

"I was in stone," she interrupted.

"That was a petrifying spell. Completely

different things." He tried to pull her against him once more.

Jennifer resisted so she could look at him more fully. "So if we love each other, and we're together, does that mean I have centuries to wait?"

The prospect of being forced to live on edge for so long out of fear of killing the man she loved was horrifying.

"Ya haven't said ya love me," he answered, his voice low.

"Everyone keeps saying it for me." She couldn't help her wry smile.

"I won't believe it until I hear it from ya." He leaned closer. His hand worked against her shoulder, pulling her gently toward him for a kiss.

"I love—"

Jim yelped, startling them.

They turned to see his little back paws disappear into the trees as he ran away from them.

"Crap." Jennifer thrust her sandwich into Rory's hand and jumped up from the bench. "I'll get him."

She automatically chased the dog.

"Jennifer, wait!" Rory called. She could hear him running after her.

Her attention focused on following the sound of Jim's feet. As she came around a curve in the dirt path, she saw him ahead of her digging into the ground. She slowed her pace and tried to calm her breathing as she went to fetch him.

"Dammit, Ji—" Something caught her back foot, and she stumbled.

When her front foot hit the ground to right herself, it too became caught. She flung her arms for balance as she felt herself starting to sink into the forest floor.

"Rory!" she yelled.

"Where…?" He appeared behind her.

Jim stopped digging and now watched them.

"Careful, it's muddy. My feet are stuck." She looked for an overhead branch to pull herself out. The more she struggled, the deeper she sank. It enveloped her calves. "Rory?"

"I'm here. Try not to move," Rory ordered. "I'll find a way to get ya out."

Jim barked.

"Ugh, it smells like rotten eggs." Jennifer gagged.

"Sulfur," he answered.

"Sulfur? Isn't that what they say demons give off in haunting movies?" Jennifer began to panic in earnest. She pushed at the ground, but her hands came back muddy. She tried to pull on her thigh to dislodge a leg. The other leg sank past her knee.

"Jennifer, stop fighting it," Rory called. She

heard him rustling around behind her. "Sulfur as in a peat bog. The smell gives it away—sulfur and methane."

"What is a peat bog doing in Wisconsin?" It was a little difficult not to panic, seeing how the earth was trying to swallow her whole. "I thought those were all in the moors of Scotland or something."

"That is what you're concerned about? With everything ya have seen of magick, Wisconsin peatlands is what ya question? There are kettle holes all over North Wisconsin."

"Kettle-what?" She tried not to panic. Her heart beat fast, and she found it difficult to breathe.

"Peatland borders kettle lakes," he said, his voice strained. "They normally feel squishy and unsteady when ya walk over them, like a layer of water is under the ground."

"I have no idea why you're telling me any of this." Jennifer tried to turn to look at him. "What are you doing?"

"I'm distracting ya so ya quit struggling," he said. "I'm going to get as close as I can and pull ya out with this branch. There is no way to tell how big this sinkhole thing is."

Jim barked again.

"What branch?" Jennifer asked. "I can't see it."

"Stay back, little buddy," Rory ordered. She heard a stick whack on the ground behind her.

"Can't you just magick me out?" she asked. The bog became colder the deeper she went.

"I don't want to alarm ya, but my magick is not working at the moment." Rory whacked the ground again, coming closer.

Was she mistaken, or did she detect fear in his voice?

Jim barked again and bounded toward Jennifer.

"No, Jim, bad dog! Sit," she yelled, trying to scare him back.

Jim's paws dented the ground as he neared her. His curious expression said he didn't understand (or care about) the command.

"Rory, get ready for Jim!" Jennifer held out her hands as the puppy approached. The second she touched fur, she grabbed Jim by the waist and lifted him from the mud. She tried to twist her body and lightly tossed him toward Rory and out of harm's way. The dog landed safely, but unfortunately, the movement tilted her back, and she sank deeper. Her left hip was sucked under, and soon her side followed. She tried to keep her hand up, but her arm and shoulder were next to go under.

"Rory?" Jennifer felt tears streaming hot across her temple. "Any time now."

"Grab the stick," Rory ordered.

She had thought being held prisoner in a petrifying spell would be the worst feeling of her life but being sucked into a grave was worse. Much worse.

Jennifer reached as Rory thrust a stick in her direction. She grabbed hold with both hands, ready to be pulled to safety.

"I got ya, love," Rory said. "Don't let go."

Jennifer held on tight. She felt her body coming out of the bog. "It's work—"

Another force countered Rory's rescue, and in the span of one breath, the earth engulfed her completely. She heard Rory yell for her. The stick ripped from her hands, and her head became encased in thick darkness. The sound of her frantic heartbeat thumped in her ears.

*Thump-thump. Thump-thump. Thump-thump.*

Jennifer tried pushing her arms to swim toward the surface, but the mud was too thick. Her lungs begged for air, warring with her tight lips as they tried to keep out the peat. Any moment, the lungs would win, and on reflex, she'd try with her last seconds to breathe.

Rory flew back as Jennifer released the stick. He landed hard on the ground. Jim ran up to him, ready to play.

Rory kept the puppy from climbing onto his stomach and pushed up from the ground. Without concern for his own safety, he leaped close to where Jennifer had disappeared. The bog caught his legs, but he didn't care as he reached into the disrupted surface. If she died, he died. There was no living without her.

"Take me, Jenny Greentooth," Rory yelled. "Not her. Take me. I'm the one ya want!"

He dug into the bog, flinging layers aside before finally punching his hand into the depths. His legs sunk deeper. Jim barked.

"Back, Jim," Rory ordered. He flung his dirty hand out of habit, trying to keep the dog safe, but his magick was useless. The puppy ran toward him, but he didn't sink into the mud, just like the child that had pushed him down all those centuries ago.

Pieces of the memory came back to him as he desperately searched for Jennifer. He'd been here before, helpless in the bog as a woman drowned in the mud.

Before, it had been a stranger. This was Jennifer. He could not lose her.

Not his Jennifer.

"Take me, Jenny, take me," he begged. "I'm the one you've been after."

Rory sank lower. Jennifer would not be able to hold her breath much longer. He was running out of time.

"Take me. Take me. Take me."

Rory screamed in frustration as he reached deeper, bringing the mud to his shoulder. His fingers bumped against something, and he grabbed hold. His fingers slipped, but he clutched his fist as tight as he could and pulled. The action caused the bog to pull his body into its depths, but he didn't care. If Jenny accepted his trade, then he would die a thousand times for the chance to save Jennifer.

Rory managed to grab hold of what felt like an arm with both hands. He pulled harder, crying out as he lifted her. The mud came to his chest now. It became difficult to breathe as the pressure of it pushed against him.

The arm he held slipped, but he would not let go. A muddy hand broke the surface.

"I have ya, my love." Rory grunted at the effort it took to pull her from the bog. "I…"

A second hand came through the surface on its own, slapping down on the ground near his face. The claws were unmistakable. It wasn't Jennifer.

"No!" The agonized cry escaped him. That was all the fight he had left.

Mud touched his jaw. The bony arm slipped from his grasp.

Peat clung to Jenny Greentooth's head. Clumps flew from her missing nose as she hissed out air. She opened her mouth and gurgled a horrible sound in his direction. Like the bog she lived in, her body looked eaten away by rot and decay. She crawled out of the muck, using the top of his head for support as she pushed him down.

The cold bog enveloped him. Rory tried to swim toward where Jennifer went under, desperate to push her to the surface. It was no use. If he could manage to move even an inch closer to her, he'd take it. If this is what eternity had in store, he would die knowing he spent it with the love of his life.

## Chapter Eighteen

Death was cold.

It was dark.

And the fear still lingered.

Jennifer's lungs had stopped fighting for air. That was how she knew she died. The taste of peat sat in her mouth like a bite of dead leaves. If she thought being stuck as a statue for a few hours was dreadful, how was she going to last forever here in the darkness?

Had she led such a bad life that this was her punishment?

*"All it takes is a dash of destiny, and everything can change."*

Was this her destiny all along? Had she been drifting toward this moment?

So much tragedy. It rushed over her. Her brother's death had led to her mother's absence. Her father's illness had fallen upon her shoulders. She didn't regret caring for him, but she hated losing him. Then came the loneliness and struggle to pay bills.

Life had not been easy, but she had not lived it badly. She didn't deserve this.

What did she deserve?

There was something….

Someone…

Rory.

She wanted Rory.

She thought of his smile, and the cold didn't feel so cold. She imagined his laugh, so real it felt as if he was trapped next to her. This would be the thought she carried into eternity—Rory, and all they could have been together.

The idea triggered her imagination, and she felt Rory against her flesh. He was part of her, in her, and she was in him wherever he was.

Jennifer saw his life as an observer in a dream. She saw him moving through time. He walked through tall grasses. His hand danced along the tops as he pushed through them, each brush of his palm like a caress. She witnessed him running after a woman, into danger. She felt his despair when he'd watched her sink into the earth. He had tried to save her with no thought of himself.

It was then Jennifer understood what happened in this enchanted bog. Sinners were encased in darkness. This was a place of judgment. The bog witch collected souls, but only those who proved themselves worthy of her punishment. Jenny Greentooth planted them in the soil, and they churned and rotted to nourish the peat.

Rory didn't deserve to be here. He'd come into the bog to rescue a stranger, and Jenny had wanted to take him, for she was greedy and wanted her souls, but she'd been unable to keep him planted. He had not been worthy of her garden. The clarity of seeing Rory's life laid out before her made Jennifer convinced of that fact. He was a good man with a kind soul. His selflessness had protected him. All those years ago in Ireland, Jenny had marked his soul so that it would find his way back to her judgment.

If Jenny needed a soul, then Jennifer would let the bog witch have hers. She would take Rory's place.

Jennifer felt movement near her head. Sharp nails scratched her scalp as someone grabbed hold of her hair and pulled. The thick mud released her from its prison as she was brought into the light. She gagged, expelling filth from her mouth, just like in the cheese-induced acid trip. She tried to see, but mud stung her eyes.

Someone's breathing sounded like a cross between a death rattle and the rasp of a heavy smoker. Her rescuer dragged her from the bog by her hair. When her hand broke free, Jennifer swiped clumps of peat from her vision. Her legs pulled from the muck with a terrible sticking sound. Once free of the bog, she slid much faster. The hold on her hair hurt, but she didn't care if it meant safety.

Suddenly, her head thumped against the ground as her rescuer dropped her. Jennifer weakly reached out as a creature stepped past her. She made contact with a leg, causing the decrepit woman to turn her attention downward.

Jenny Greentooth.

Jennifer instantly let go. The hunched, bony frame looked as if it might have once been human. Long stringy hair clung to the bog witch's back. Mud coated her naked, wrinkled flesh like paint.

"Rory," Jennifer whispered, unable to scream for him like she wanted.

Jenny's unfortunate, noseless face pressed close. The raspy breathing was louder now, joined by the foulness of her breath.

"Rory," Jennifer repeated. "Take me for Rory."

The words seemed to annoy the witch, and she growled. Jennifer flinched, but Jenny didn't touch her again. She merely stood and continued back to the bog.

Jim barked in excitement and ran past her. Jennifer pushed up, trying to grab the puppy but missed it. He pranced after Jenny. The bog witch ignored the dog.

"Rory?" Jennifer called a little louder. She couldn't see him. He wouldn't have left her behind. There was only one place he could be.

Jennifer crawled after Jenny.

Jenny flung her arms, grumbling and growling as she clawed her way into the earth. Suddenly, she thrust her hand inside the small hole she'd made and turned. With one hand, she dragged Rory from the bog toward Jennifer. Her hunched body didn't appear to labor under the task. Once he was free from the hole, Jenny dropped him on the ground near Jennifer.

"Rory?" Jennifer swiped the mud from his face, digging past his lips to remove it from his mouth.

For several very long seconds, his chest did not move. She didn't want to breathe mud into his lungs but didn't know what else to do. She pressed her mouth to his and prepared to force air into him.

Rory's hand pressed into her face, stopping her. She looked down to see his handsome eyes gazing up at her. She exhaled sharply in relief.

"Rory," she whispered. "Oh, thank goodness."

She glanced up to see Jenny standing in the disrupted soil. Her body was slowly sinking into the earth.

"Thank you," Jennifer said, too weak to stand and unwilling to leave Rory's side.

Jenny's answer was anything but pleasant. The bog witch opened her mouth wide and let out a horrible screech.

"Jennifer?" Rory's voice came on a pant.

Jennifer kept her hand on his chest to feel him breathing but watched Jenny as she disappeared into the ground.

"How?" Rory asked, his hand slipping over hers on his chest.

"She let us go," Jennifer said, finally looking at him. "We weren't worthy of her garden."

"I don't know what that means and don't care." Rory cupped her face. "I thought I lost ya, love. I thought…"

His words choked a little, and tears entered his eyes.

"I thought you lost me too there for a

moment." Jennifer couldn't keep herself upright and dropped down next to him. She rested on her side as he still held her hand to his chest over the comforting beat of his heart. "But it's over now. She's gone."

Rory's brow furrowed as he rolled onto his stomach. Her hand slid off him. He pulled himself to his feet and stumbled toward the bog. Cautiously, he stepped forward, tapping his toe until he crossed the now-dried path.

"I don't think she's coming back." Jennifer watched him from her place on the ground. Her eyes stung with small granules of dirt, and she had to close them.

"I don't understand. Why did Jenny let us go?" Rory came back to her. She felt more than saw him.

"Has your magick returned? Can you conjure some water so I can clean out my eyes?" Jennifer asked.

"I can do one better." Rory ran her hand over her face. Energy tingled her flesh as he used his magick. The mud flaked away from her skin, clearing her eyes and nose. The taste of peat disappeared from her mouth.

"Oh, thank you," she said.

Rory hooked his arm under her armpit and helped her to her feet.

She chuckled in relief. "I was afraid I was going to have to kiss you with the worst case of morning peat breath in history."

Rory did the same to his face, cleaning the mud from it with magick. "I'd do more, but I'm afraid my magick is drained."

The mud still stuck to their hair and clothes, but Jennifer didn't care. They were alive. They were breathing and…

"I love you," Jennifer stated. "When Jim ran off, I was trying to tell you. I love you."

"We need to buy that puppy a leash." Rory kissed her gently before whispering, "Say it again."

"I love you." She smiled.

"Again." He pressed his cheek to hers.

"I love you," she whispered.

"I will never tire of hearing that," he said with a soft moan.

"I will never stop saying it," she promised.

Rory glanced back to where Jenny had departed. "I should get ya back to the house."

"I don't think she's planning to return. We're not worthy of her garden," Jennifer said.

"Ya mentioned that before, but what do ya mean garden?" Rory swooped his arm around Jim and carried him like a tiny football as he urged Jennifer to walk with him toward the mansion.

"The bog, you said it's enchanted," she explained.

"Aye."

"I think it's like purgatory or some kind of afterlife." Jennifer hugged close to Rory, still chilly from their ordeal. The mud made her clothes heavy and uncomfortable. "When I was in there I understood. It showed me things."

"What kinds of things?" Rory brought the wiggling puppy closer to his chest and held him. The animal's fur became matted.

"I saw you. I saw a lot of you. It's like I watched your life over the years like the bog was trying to decide if you deserved to be there if it could use you."

"Use me for what?"

"Fuel for Jenny's garden. She can't keep you unless you earned your place. When you went after that woman, that selfless act saved you. But you're magickal and strong, and Jenny wanted that for herself. She marked you with a curse so she could try again. It was my destiny to find you and bring you to judgment."

"No, it was your destiny to find me, but not for judgment." He kissed her gently. "It's because you're the other half of my heart."

"And you're mine," she answered. Jennifer

stopped walking and tried to catch her breath. "Sorry. I need a moment."

"Take as long as ya need." Even as he said it, he looked worried as he peered down the way they'd come.

"I felt Jenny's rage when she couldn't have you the first time. The blade would have transported your soul to her. When that didn't work, she brought the bog to us. I saw your life, Rory. You're a good man. Jenny saw that too. That's why she couldn't keep you." Jennifer gave a small laugh. "I think it pissed her off, to be honest. If I'm not mistaken, she was pouting as she was pulling us from the sludge."

She nudged his arm to prompt him to walk with her again.

"If ya saw my life, maybe ya are the one who judged me." Rory's lip curled with a half-smile, and she wondered what he was thinking.

"I want it noted for the record that I'm human. I'm not a bog witch, or wench, or descendent of one. For whatever reason, my name being similar to hers was enough to connect us. That's it."

"Noted, but it wouldn't matter to me if you were a bog witch," Rory answered.

"I'm human," she insisted.

"It makes sense. There is power in a name, in

words. Spells are created with them all the time. If what ya say is true, then Jenny was waiting for the right combination of factors so her curse could play out."

Jim tried to lick Rory's dirty hand, and he pulled it out of reach.

"Just so we're all clear on the me being human part," she said. "Be sure to tell the elders, so they stop calling me names and trying to potion me. I can promise I won't lose my temper if they start up again."

"I like that. It sounds like we have a future." His grin widened. "I'd kneel, but I'm not sure I'd be capable of standing back up."

"Kneel? For what?" Jennifer glanced at the ground.

"For this." Rory kissed her again, slow and deep. She felt him all the way to her toes. When he broke the kiss, he said, "Marry me, love. When I thought I lost ya I knew that I would never be able to live without ya. If ya have truly seen my life, then ya know everything ya need to know. And if ya don't, I'll tell ya the rest."

"I did see quite a bit." Jennifer studied his face. "Including that little incident with Lady Sylvia back in the 1700s. I can't say I am happy to have that memory thrust into my brain. I saw you checking out her backside."

Rory's eyes widened, and he began to sputter a little. "Now, my love, ya can't be mad about that. Ya weren't even born yet. She meant nothing to me. No other woman existed before ya. Not really. I—"

Jennifer laughed. "You're way too easy to tease."

"I…" He looked confused, as if unsure if he was in trouble.

"Yes, Mr. MacGregor. I'll marry you." Jennifer closed her eyes and offered her mouth. She felt Jim squirming in protest as he squeezed lightly between them. When she pulled back, she gazed into Rory's eyes and whispered, "But seriously, do you think you can sneak us into a shower? If your family sees me like this, I'm never living the bog witch nickname down."

## Chapter Nineteen

IRELAND, SIX WEEKS LATER...

Jennifer stood in the field of rocky protrusions and wildflowers. The long white skirt of her wedding dress clung to her legs in the breeze. The gown was simple, but not as simple as she would have chosen. Cait and Margareta had been overly helpful in the wedding planning.

Jennifer saw no hint of what had transpired there hundreds of years ago when she looked over the beautiful landscape. But she knew. She recognized a feeling radiating from the place, though the enchanted bog was no longer there. Part of her expected to see Jenny Greentooth pop her head up from the ground to witness the nuptials.

"Ya are the loveliest vision." Rory stood next to her in his formal kilt. "My life truly began the moment I saw ya."

In the last few weeks, she'd learned a lot about his family's traditions. One is that they took their kilt fashion very seriously. His brother, cousins, uncles, and father all stood nearby with matching attire. The women had opted for nicer dresses. Since Jennifer didn't have family, Maura stood up for her as a bridesmaid. Their flower girl, Jewel, wore leather pants, a vest, and a plastic sword. They'd tried to put her in a princess dress, but she kept magickally changing her outfit into that of her new favorite playtime character, a dragon slayer.

"This is where it all started," Jennifer said. "All it takes is a dash of destiny, and everything can change. Our destiny was written in this earth centuries years ago, and it is here I pledge my love to you for the rest of eternity. I am yours. Forever."

The vows weren't traditional, but they were hers, and they were real. Jennifer didn't need a flowery speech to tell Rory how she felt. She showed him her love every single day.

"Forever," he repeated.

Rory brought his mouth to hers, kissing her deeply. She felt his magick inside of her as if it were her own.

"Och, we're not to that part, laddie," Murdoch said.

"Let them be. I declare them married." Raibeart sniffed.

"Are ya crying?" Angus asked.

"Aye, mayhap a little," Raibeart answered. "It's romantic. Let's move this party to the pub. Ladies love wedding parties. Puts them in the mood for lovemaking."

Cheering and clapping erupted, causing them to break their kiss.

"Welcome to the family!" Murdoch pulled Jennifer away from her new husband and gave her a giant hug. She found herself passed around from father to uncle to brother to sister to cousins to aunts as they all congratulated her.

Yeah, they could be a bit overwhelming at times.

Rory rescued her as he swooped her up into his arms and began carrying her away from the field.

"Follow me!" Raibeart declared. "I know the way."

"Liquor is the other way," Murdoch said when Raibeart would march them into the wilderness.

Raibeart instantly turned and thrust his hand into the air. "To the liquor!"

"Well, at least he's wearing clothes," Jane told her husband.

"For now," Lydia answered as she threaded

her arm into Erik's. "The evening is young, and I have a feeling Ireland is about to have several reports of invading naked Scots."

"Jewel, no," Andrea yelled. "No dragon! No dragon!"

Jennifer glanced into the sky just in time to see a mythical beast disappear into a puff of smoke. She inhaled sharply and held tighter to her new husband.

"Don't worry. You're a MacGregor now. You'll get used to it," Rory said.

"I made a cake," Cait announced to the family.

Jennifer buried her head in Rory's shoulder and whispered, "Yeah, that's scarier than the dragon. I'm still not eating anything your mother gives me."

The End

## The Series Continues

WARLOCKS MACGREGOR® 9: NIGHT MAGICK

Maura MacGregor might by new to the secretly magickal town of Green Vallis, but this isn't her first dance with the devil. See what fate has in store for her!

*Warning: Contains yummy, hot, mischievous MacGregors who are almost certainly up to no good on their quest to find true love. And Uncle Raibeart.*

For more information, visit
www.MichellePillow.com

## Warlocks MacGregor® Series

SCOTTISH MAGICKAL WARLOCKS

Love Potions

Spellbound

Stirring Up Trouble

Cauldrons and Confessions

Spirits and Spells

Kisses and Curses

Magick and Mischief

A Dash of Destiny

Night Magick

**More Coming Soon**

Visit www.MichellePillow.com for details.

## Newsletter

To stay informed about when a new book in the series installments is released, sign up for updates:

Sign up for Michelle's Newsletter
michellepillow.com/author-updates

## About Michelle M. Pillow

*New York Times* & *USA TODAY*
**Bestselling Author**

Michelle loves to travel and try new things, whether it's a paranormal investigation of an old Vaudeville Theatre or climbing Mayan temples in Belize. She believes life is an adventure fueled by copious amounts of coffee.

Newly relocated to the American South, Michelle is involved in various film and documentary projects with her talented director husband. She is mom to a fantastic artist. And she's managed by a dog and cat who make sure she's meeting her deadlines.

For the most part she can be found wearing pajama pants and working in her office. There may or may not be dancing. It's all part of the creative process.

**Come say hello! Michelle loves talking
with readers on social media!**

www.MichellePillow.com

facebook.com/AuthorMichellePillow

twitter.com/michellepillow

instagram.com/michellempillow

bookbub.com/authors/michelle-m-pillow

goodreads.com/Michelle_Pillow

amazon.com/author/michellepillow

youtube.com/michellepillow

pinterest.com/michellepillow

## Complimentary Material

# Dragon Prince (Qurilixen Lords)

### BY MICHELLE M. PILLOW

*Grier's fiery passion for Salena might be everything his dragon ever wanted but loving her might just lead to the destruction of everything he's trying to save.*

With all that is happening in his land, the upcoming shifter mating ceremony is the least of Grier's concerns. Even though he is heir prince of the dragon-shifters, he doesn't have the authority needed to help the humans stranded in dragon territory, nor can he banish those who ruthlessly control them. Yet honor demands he finds an opportunity to intervene, and he hopes that doing so won't start a war the shifters can't win. Discovering his destined mate couldn't have come at a worse time.

Salena knows what it is like to be a pawn of

the Federation. They might have kidnapped her and brought her to this strange territory, but she will never do what they want of her... what everyone wants of her. The last thing the fugitive needs is the very public attention of a fierce dragon prince claiming they're fated by the gods —even if the sexy man makes her burn in more ways than one.

---

## Dragon Prince Exclusive Excerpt

Shouts sounded from below. Grier narrowed his gaze to focus his vision as his eyes shifted to make out the details. A mob of people flowed through the central street of the city, clashing with a second mob. The people converged like two swollen streams, spilling over into the side streets.

He sighed heavily. The fighting was not unusual.

Grier resisted the urge to swoop down and drag them apart with his talons. Instead, he went to the side of the roof, grabbed a knob that had been placed at the edge, and then dropped over the side. He swung around into an opening at the top of the tower and landed on the stone floor. There, he pulled off his boots and pants. Once naked, he went to the window and dove from the tower. His body fell for a few seconds before he let the shift have him. The transformation was painful, but it was an old pain that he had long ago learned to disregard.

Grier's bones cracked as his body extended, and his skin hardened with protective brown armor. Wings ripped out of his back, lifting him before he hit the ground. The transformation finished as he was suspended in the air. A long tail grew from the bottom of his spine only to have a spade sharpen the end. Deadly talons replaced his nails. His beard disappeared, and his jaw popped, making room for sharp teeth.

The wind caressed the full length of his form. For a moment, the feeling of freedom rushed through him, the animal instinct desperate to take over his reason. The beast was as much a part of him as the man. He pushed the feeling down, concentrating on what needed to be done.

Grier dove toward the fight in the street, roaring before sending a burst of flames into the sky. He was careful not to hit any of the structures, but it was enough to get the people's attention. He swooped over the epicenter of the hostility. Screams pierced the air as people ran away from him to take cover.

Grier roared once in warning before lifting

himself higher and flying away. Then, because the freedom of flight felt so damned good, he circled the entire city a few times before heading back to the tower. He wanted to keep soaring but forced himself to land on the roof.

His body contracted as he shifted halfway back to his human form to stand as a dragon-man. It was in this half shift that he looked like his father's dragon. The tail disappeared as did the talons on his feet. The talons on his fingers shortened, still sharp and deadly but more like fingernails. In this form, the dragon impulses were easier to control. He used his dragon vision to look down at the valley below. The fighting had dispersed, and the streets cleared of both mobs. The fray was over.

The thick armor of Grier's skin protected his naked body as he slid down the side of the roof. He again grabbed the knob and swung down into the tower window. His clothes were piled on the floor. Now safely inside, the armored flesh softened into human skin, and he again stood as a man.

The tight pants felt a little constrictive after a shift. His sensitive skin tingled. Grier leaned against the partition wall as he tugged on his boots before rounding the corner to the other side. The wall acted like a windshield for the landing room.

Stacks of plain linen shirts and pants had little by way of style but were cheap to make. They served as replacement clothes for the flyers, and he took a shirt from the top of the pile. Their full dragon bodies expanded beyond the confines of clothing. It was a little hard to fit a giant pair of wings into a tunic shirt, and they'd kept ending up naked in inopportune situations.

His aunt Olena had been the one to suggest the caches around the kingdom. Out of all the elders, she alone never tried to curb their wild ways. It wasn't a secret in their family that she'd been somewhat of a space pirate in her youth. She used to hide treasures in the forest for them to hunt down.

Grace had set his thoughts toward the past when he needed to think about the present. The tension in Shelter City had already spilled over into the rest of the planet. The little skirmish below was bad, but it was hardly the worst. Some of the residents were trying to migrate, especially those who'd been born since their arrival.

The Federation didn't like that. In fact, they had forbidden Cysgodians from leaving the city limits.

The Cysgodians' desire to be part of the Qurilixian culture wasn't an issue for the shifters.

Dragons would always do the honorable thing and these people needed a place to live.

He gripped the shirt in his hands as he took the winding path down the stairs. There was little light to see by, but his shifted eyes didn't need help to navigate the way down. Even though the fight was broken up, he should go to the city and find out what had started it.

A soft glow caught his attention, and he turned around to see who followed him. No one was there. He looked down the steps—again, nothing unusual. It was then he realized what caused the glow.

The crystal on his wrist had begun to pulsate with a soft light.

Grier held very still, unable to believe what was happening. He took another step down, then stopped, unsure what he should do. How could his mating crystal be glowing if he was alone in the tower?

He was alone, wasn't he?

Did he really want to find the answer to that question?

"Show yourself," he ordered.

Silence.

His crystal was only meant to glow if he was close to his mate. It was the belief of his people. When they were born, their fathers dove to the bottom of Crystal Lake and chose a crystal. That stone stayed with them until they married. No one was one hundred percent sure how it worked, but they knew that it did. There was no questioning the will of the gods.

"By order of the prince, show yourself," he commanded.

His heartbeat quickened. Had the gods heard him tell his cousin he had no wish to marry? Had they taken offense to his rejection of their gifts and this was their answer to his blasphemy?

Grier ran down the stairs. He couldn't be alone with a glowing crystal. It would mean he was cursed. There was no other explanation.

"Who is there?" Desperation made the dragon's gruff nature enter his voice.

He rushed out the tower, hearing the weight of the wood door slam shut behind him. The rocky landscape was empty as Grier ran around the base of the tower to see if a woman hid from him. His feet slipped as he came close to the edge of the cliff. Pebbles fell down the side, clanking to punctuate how alone he was.

"Please, someone be there," he whispered into the wind. "Where are you? Show yourself."

The glow of his crystal faded. He lifted his arm, pointing the bracelet in every direction to see if the crystal would reactivate. It was over.

In those brief seconds, everything changed.

Grier forgot about the village squabble. How could he think of such things now? He'd received an answer to his offhanded comment to Grace. He would be forever alone.

The gods had cursed him for his arrogance.

**To find out more about Michelle's books visit www.MichellePillow.com**

## Please Leave a Review

THANK YOU FOR READING!

Please take a moment to share your thoughts by reviewing this book.

Be sure to check out Michelle's other titles at
www.MichellePillow.com

CPSIA information can be obtained
at www.ICGtesting.com
Printed in the USA
LVHW031032281220
675212LV00023B/233

9 781625 012586